A SECOND CHANCE

THE KELLER FAMILY SERIES ~ BOOK TWO

BERNADETTE MARIE

5 PRINCE PUBLISHING

4th Edition 2021

Published by 5 Prince Publishing, PO Box 865, Arvada, CO 80001

www.5PrinceBooks.com

Digital ISBN 13: 9780985334550

Print ISBN: 978-1-63112-021-3

For Stan
For loving me and each and every little flaw.

ACKNOWLEDGMENTS

For all *my* men who stand behind everything I do. I thank you. I am honored to have you in my life. To Mom, Dad, and Anni, without you I'd have no foundation in which to build lovable families. Susan, having you as my friend, even when you are marking up my work, brings me such joy.

For Connie, who was very candid in sharing her battle with plasma cancer, and who always kept her spirits high and encourages me daily. You have been an asset in my personal (and professional) life.

For my Aunt Bev, who will forever amaze me with her kind heart, soft words, gentle ways, and ability to comfort others, even as she faced her own challenges. May I walk as gracefully as you do some day.

For Melissa. Our time together on this planet was very short. But the memory of you is forever imbedded in my heart. No child should ever have to go through what you went through, but because of you I cherish every moment I have with my own children. And to Teri, her mother, you cross my mind almost daily now that I am a parent. I see your strength now that I have endured so many things with my sons. Your strong spirit, and the memory of your husband and daughter, stays with me and I cherish the time we were neighbors and friends.

For Lisa. I will forever laugh that I thought you shaved your head because you had a bad haircut. I never would have assumed that breast cancer would forever shadow your life. Thank you for being there for me when I needed you. Thank you for the food, companionship, and friendship. Thank you for watching my kids and cleaning my house, when really you probably didn't feel good at all. Years later, thank you for intimately sharing your story with me so that Madeline could become more realistic. And above all else, thank you for being my friend.

ALSO BY BERNADETTE MARIE

THE MATCHMAKER SERIES

Matchmakers

Encore

Finding Hope

THE THREE MRS. MONROES TRILOGY

Amelia

Penelope

Vivian

THE ASPEN CREEK SERIES

First Kiss

Unexpected Admirer

On Thin Ice

Indomitable Spirit

THE DENVER BRIDE SERIES

Cart Before the Horse

Never Saw it Coming

Candy Kisses

ROMANTIC SUSPENSE

Chasing Shadows

PARANORMAL ROMANCES

The Tea Shop

The Last Goodbye

HOLIDAY FAVORITES

Corporate Christmas

Tropical Christmas

Date for Hire

A SECOND CHANCE

CHAPTER 1

*A*t the end of the long, tree-lined drive stood the house, welcoming her just as the owner would. It wasn't the first time Madeline Carson had made the trip out to Regan and Zach Benson's house, but she couldn't help but wonder if it would be the last.

She batted back the tears that stung her eyes. No, she wasn't going to cry for herself. She was there to celebrate the birth of Regan's baby boy. Tyler Alan Benson. A child welcomed into the world by two people who were so very much in love.

Oh, she was adult enough to admit she was jealous. Who wouldn't be? Zach doted on his wife of three years. A baby would only enhance the perfect relationship that her ex-sister-in-law had with her husband.

There had been a time when she'd felt that optimism about a man, love, and her family.

The first tear fell.

It had been five years since she and Carlos Keller, Regan's brother, had divorced. Five years, and she still mourned it every day.

After her marriage to Carlos ended, there was his best friend,

1

Matt. He'd been there to console her in her time of need. That need had led to a relationship, and they'd married only six months after her divorce had been finalized.

The marriage had ended the twenty-year friendship between Matt and Carlos, but who could blame them?

Neither Carlos nor Madeline could really pinpoint what went wrong to end their marriage. It simply had fallen apart. There were money issues, of course. Then the kids came along, and the money was even tighter as Carlos finished graduate school and she worked two jobs. The very things that were to have made their family stronger had actually pulled it apart.

Matt hadn't meant any harm when he had come to console her. He was playing the part of a friend to each of them. Things simply had changed between him and Madeline, and they'd fallen in love. Or so she'd thought at the time.

Madeline pulled to the side of the driveway and wiped at her eyes.

No, it hadn't been love. It had been comfort. Matt needed to take care of someone, and she was willing to let him take care of her. He'd let her stay home and raise her children. She couldn't have asked for more.

Now even that had fallen apart.

Madeline glanced at the messenger bag on the passenger seat. Inside it were the divorce papers that Matt had served her with three days ago. So far, she hadn't had the courage to sign them. She hadn't even had the courage to discuss it with her children. They would get to that. As soon as Carlos brought them back to her after his week with them, they'd realize Matt had moved out. She'd like to think they'd be a little upset that he was gone, but she knew they wouldn't.

Oh, it would hurt for the moment. It would hurt more because they'd know it hurt her, but they were too in love with their father to want another man in their lives, or hers.

Sure, Matt had been a good role model and a loving man to

them all. He simply wasn't their father. For the first time in days, she smiled through her tears. Her children loved their father and he loved them.

She took a few cleansing breaths. Matt's leaving couldn't have come at a worse time. Having your husband walk out on you never happened at a convenient time, but she had a bigger battle to face now.

Madeline put her hand to her chest and looked down at the swells of her breasts against her shirt.

She had cancer and she hadn't told a soul.

Sadness filled her body with a heavy fullness, and anger riddled her mind. Madeline had never imagined this would happen to her.

"Well, now isn't the time to sob over your sad life," she said to herself as she pulled down the visor and looked in the mirror. She wiped off the smudged mascara and fixed her hair. "This is Regan's moment. It's time to celebrate life."

Once she successfully pulled herself together, she started toward the house.

The chairs on the porch rocked in the breeze. The November air had chilled, but the ground was still dry. That would be changing soon, she thought as she parked the car.

Madeline looked at the house. It had been Zach's engagement present to Regan. Or, as Regan referred to it, her bribe to marry him, which had worked in his favor. Over the past three years, Regan had added her touches. In the spring, the flowers would all bloom around the porch and lay out a colorful spread of welcome. As it was, the drive was paved with leaves that had finally given up their homes on the branches of the trees that lined the road.

She climbed from the car and opened the trunk. The large box she'd brought for Regan and Zach sat wrapped in bright yellow paper, reminding her that a new life was just beyond those doors. A cousin to her children, a nephew to her ex-husband, and a blessing to Regan and Zach.

She lifted the box from the trunk and moved it to her hip. Then she shut the trunk, walked up the front steps, and pushed the doorbell. When she heard it chime, she realized that she'd probably woken the baby.

Regan pulled open the door and smiled. "Madeline. I'm so glad you were able to come by. Please, come in." She stood back to let her through.

"You look wonderful," she said, but she saw the signs of motherhood streaked across poor Regan's face. Her eyes were hollow and dark from lack of sleep. The elegant attire worn by the wife of one of Tennessee's most prominent businessmen had been swapped for a pair of comfy sweat pants and an oversized T-shirt to encompass her swollen breasts. "This is for you and Tyler." She handed the box to Regan.

"You didn't have to do this."

"It's a box of necessities. Diapers. Diaper-rash cream. Nipple cream for the mama."

"Thank you," Regan said on a sigh.

"Just a few other things I think you can use up. I didn't buy him any clothes. I figured Zach's mother would want to do most of that."

"You're right. Audrey will make sure he's the best-dressed child at the playground. I think she cleaned out the Baby Gap." She shook her head. "Zach tells her to quit buying him things, he's only a week old, but she insists."

"I'd have to agree. Grandmothers get special rights."

"Would you like to see him?" Regan offered.

"Of course."

Regan laced her arm through Madeline's and escorted her to the living room. Madeline smiled when she saw the bassinet near the sofa with the sleeping baby. Her heart ached a bit with the memory of all of her own children sleeping in it. "Your mother gave you the bassinet?"

"Yes, she wants everyone to have a chance to sleep in it. Carlos and Arianna were the only two of her own children that didn't get to."

The Keller family was an eclectic mix, Madeline thought. Regan and Arianna had been adopted by the Kellers, but had been with them since Regan was an infant and Arianna was two years old. Their little brother, Curtis, was the Kellers' only natural-born child, and he was a year younger than Regan. Carlos had been adopted by Emily and Alan Keller when he was seven, after a car accident had killed his parents.

When Madeline had given birth to Eduardo, Emily gave her and Carlos the bassinet for their children. Now it was Tyler's turn. "I guess Clara was the last one to sleep in it," Madeline reminisced.

"I can't believe she's eleven."

"Tell me about it. The boys are both teenagers." She looked at Regan. "I'm not that old, am I?"

Regan touched her arm. "Heavens, no."

They laughed, but when Tyler stirred, they both stopped and watched.

"I fed him only fifteen minutes ago. He should be pretty happy for now. Would you like to hold him?"

"Oh, Regan, he's sleeping. Don't bother him."

"Give me a break. You drove forty-five minutes out here to see him. I know you, Madeline. You came to hold the baby." Regan reached for her son. "He'll sleep just as fine in your arms as he will in that bassinet."

She adjusted the blanket around him as she handed him to Madeline.

CHAPTER 2

*M*adeline sat down on the couch with the baby, who cooed against her. "He's so perfect."

"He is, isn't he?" Regan adjusted into the corner of the couch and relaxed.

"Eduardo had hair like this." She smoothed her hand over Tyler's thick, dark hair. "Christian and Clara were both bald. Remember?" Regan nodded her answer with a yawn. "Time flies."

Madeline let Tyler wrap his tiny hand around her finger, and she felt the tug in her heart. It seemed so long ago when Carlos had sat by her side in the hospital and they admired their first baby. "I wonder if his hair will stay dark like yours or if he'll get his daddy's light hair."

"Hmmm," was all Regan said. Her head had rested to the back of the couch, and her eyes had closed.

Madeline simply smiled and sat quietly. She'd been there too. It would never cease to amaze her how mothers did it. They could go and go with no sleep and provide the essentials that their babies needed. But when exhaustion took over, it was like running right into a wall.

The struggles of motherhood were just like the cancer that

was taking over her body. In order to survive it, she would have to love herself as she loved her children. She would need to have hope, just as she had when her children became their own people and began to experience new things. And she'd need to remember to take care of herself as she'd neglected to do for the past fifteen years while she doted on her own babies. It would be easier if Carlos were there with her.

"Well, little man, you've been born into one of the most wonderful families in the world. You'll be well taken care of," she whispered, kissing him atop the head and wondering if she'd see him grow up.

"You look natural doing that," Carlos said from the doorway, watching her.

His voice startled her, and she froze, trying not to wake the baby as her heart pounded in her chest. "Dear God, you scared me to death." She tried to ease back into the couch without stirring Tyler. She looked up at the man who had once captured her heart and somehow continued to do so. His long, lean body and handfuls of wavy black hair played with her imagination too often. "How long have you been standing there?"

"A few minutes. Did you knock her out?" He nodded toward his sister.

Madeline let out a sigh. "She's so tired. I was surprised Audrey or your mother weren't here to help her."

"Yeah, right. You know Regan. She wanted to do it alone. Besides, Audrey had a hair appointment."

"Where are the kids?"

"They're putting their things in your car. I told them to stay outside so they didn't bother the baby. Clara is pouting, but the boys are fine with it."

Madeline looked back down at the sleeping baby in her arms. "Well, sweetheart, I guess I'd better go. I'm glad I got to meet you."

"You don't have to put him down. Stay as long as you'd like."

"Oh, I should get them home and settled." She rose and put Tyler back in the bassinet. She laid a kiss on her fingers and gently pressed it to his cheek. "Good-bye."

She stood from the bassinet and felt the room begin to spin around her.

"Whoa." Carlos was at her side steadying her. "Are you all right?"

"Yeah." She tried to regain her balance. "I'm fine."

"You don't look so well. Why don't you sit down?" He held tight to her arms.

"I really should be going."

"Madeline, there's no need for you to run. You're still part of this family."

She smiled and nodded. The entire Keller family had always made her feel right at home, even after she and Carlos had divorced.

Madeline took a deep breath and soaked in the feeling of Carlos' hands on her. She missed him, and that, on top of everything that was happening to her, wasn't helping her steady her emotions. Instead, his nearness and the heat of his body were stirring up feelings she had no right to have, not anymore.

"I'm okay now." She reached her hand toward his chest, but he didn't let her go.

Carlos eyes scanned over her slowly. "You're sick. You should let me call Curtis and have him come look at you."

"No." She shook her head. "You're not calling your brother to come and check up on me. I'm fine. I'm just coming down with something. All the better reason for me to go home before I get this little man sick." She looked back down at the baby sleeping in the family bassinet. The sadness inside her stirred again. What she wouldn't give to hold her children and watch them sleep with Carlos by her side once more.

Carlos steadied his eyes on hers and then stepped back. "If you need me, you call."

"I will."

"Let Matt know what happened."

Madeline nodded. Once she had turned to Matt for comfort—whom was she going to turn to now that he was gone? "Thanks for meeting me out here with the kids."

"Sure. Oh, by the way, Mom says there's still room for two more at the table on Thanksgiving. You and Matt are welcome to come."

"Thank her for me, will you? I think I'll just have a quiet Thanksgiving at home. I'll bring the kids by on Thursday morning after we watch the parade."

"The parade. Still your most favorite thing on TV?"

"And it always will be," she said, smiling, thinking about the time Carlos had maxed out every credit card they had to make sure she witnessed it live on the streets of New York. That was a lifetime ago, she reminded herself. Too bad she'd fought him over it instead of realizing the sentiment behind it.

She touched his arm as she walked past him, and then hurried out to her car where her children waited for her. Their smiles took away the pain she'd been feeling. Even when everything around her seemed to be shattering, she still had her children.

Panic suddenly filled her, and she fought back the emotions that were clawing at her. She wondered how long she had left to be their mother.

CHAPTER 3

*C*arlos waved as the car disappeared down the long drive. The pain that ripped through him each time they passed off the kids was back. It had been five years. He'd thought it would get easier, but it never did.

They'd had a family together. That was supposed to be forever.

As he walked back into the room, Regan stirred awake. "Did I fall asleep?"

"Yeah. Tyler graduated from college yesterday, and now he's getting married."

"Smart–ass." She laughed as she sat up. "I didn't mean to fall asleep while she was here. That was rude of me."

"That's what she said."

"Liar, she'd never say a mean thing ever." She looked down at her son and smiled. "He's so perfect."

"He really is. When will Zach be home?"

"He's finishing up a meeting with John Forrester. He'll be home in an hour or so."

"Will you be okay?"

"Yeah, I'm fine. Go if you need to."

He shoved his hands into the front pockets of his jeans. "Kathy's making a special dinner tonight."

"Things are going well between the two of you?" Regan tucked her feet under her and smiled up at him.

"Yeah. It's been long enough. It's time for me to move on, don't you think?"

"Only if you're ready." Her voice was soft and all too knowing.

Carlos had to be ready. It still hurt to watch Madeline live a happy life without him. He was dying inside, and he needed to find that kind of love again.

"I'm ready, Reg. I'm tired of wondering what happened to my perfect marriage. She moved on. She remarried. I need to fall in love, and I need to move on."

"And you're in love with Kathy?"

"I didn't say that." The word love twisted his gut. "I'm just willing to feel it out. I like her a lot."

"She's a nice woman."

"Good, I have my little sister's blessing." He bent to kiss her on the cheek. "Take care of my little man. Uncle Carlos will come back out tomorrow."

"You're worse than Mom," she called after him as he left the room.

"Bite your tongue," he hollered back.

THE DRIVE BACK FROM REGAN AND ZACH'S WAS LONG AND LOUD. The kids had been with their father for the week. Even though Madeline had spoken to them each night, they all had their own set of stories they wanted to tell her, and all at the same time.

Clara had aced her spelling test. Christian scored twelve points in his basketball game. Eduardo had only two hundred and forty-five days until he could drive. She smiled at him and shook her head.

"That's only if your father and I agree to it."

"He'll agree. I'd be able to help out. Just think about it, Mom. I could get everyone to school and back and forth between your house and dad's house. Really, Mom, I'm only thinking about you."

She reached across the car and laid her hand on her son's arm. These were the moments she had to fight for.

"Son, you are the most thoughtful thing."

"Kathy says that by the time he's got his license, maybe she'll be in the market for a new car," Clara offered.

Madeline swallowed hard. Kathy. She could feel the tears stinging her eyes behind her sunglasses, and she forced them back.

She was more than familiar with the name. Clara had taken to the woman, and the boys thought she was nice enough. In her heart, she knew she should be happy for her ex-husband, but she just couldn't be.

Madeline had been the one to remarry less than a year after they'd divorced. Even worse, she'd married his best friend and ruined that relationship. Now she was alone, and Carlos had finally found happiness. She deserved that, she decided. Karma was a tricky thing. You might have thought what you did was right, but in the end you end up alone and dying.

"Mom, are you okay?" Eduardo reached his hand to her shoulder.

"I'm fine, sweetie."

"You're spacing out. Want me to drive?"

"You can drive me home in two hundred and forty-five days," she said, feeling the tension in her shoulders build as they turned into their neighborhood and drove into the driveway.

Matt's car was gone, and she wondered how long it would take for one of them to notice that so was everything else Matt owned.

It took exactly sixteen minutes.

"Mom! Where is the Wii?" Christian called from the family room.

Madeline squeezed her eyes tight and took a deep breath as she stood over the sink in the kitchen.

"It's gone. It's all gone! The Wii, the games, the guitars!" He ran through the door to the kitchen. "Mom, even Matt's chair is gone. I think someone broke into the house."

Clara was right on his heels, and Eduardo flew down the stairs from his room when he heard the chaos.

Madeline sucked up her courage and straightened her spine. When she turned, three sets of dark eyes watched her. "Why don't you all sit down? Let's talk."

They didn't say another word. Madeline knew they could see the pain in her face. She'd explain everything about Matt, but until she had a solid path toward treatment, she wasn't about to mention the cancer.

She sat down at the kitchen table with her children and set her clasped hands on the top. "Matt moved out."

They said nothing, but their eyes were open wide. Clara began to cry.

Madeline swallowed hard. "He's asked me for a divorce. I have the papers and I just have to sign them."

Eduardo reached across the table and touched her hand. "Mom, why? Did we do something wrong?"

Heaviness filled her chest as she looked into her son's apologetic eyes. "Oh, no, honey. This has nothing to do with you at all. He loves you. He was most worried about all of you." She patted his hand and reached for Clara's. "Matt and I, well, we've just grown apart. After your dad and I got a divorce, we seemed to need each other. I just don't think we ever loved each other like a man and wife should. We loved each other like friends."

Clara flew from her seat and into Madeline's arms. The strength that she'd been holding on to collapsed, and she sobbed with her daughter against her chest. The softness of Clara's hair brushed against her cheek, and the strawberry scent reminded her how young her children still were. How precious. How innocent.

Eduardo stood and walked to his mother and sister. He wrapped his arms around both of them. Christian sat strong across the table and watched, as she'd known he would. He was the strong and silent one. He'd break down in his room with the door shut. When he did, she would go to him.

And when it was time, she went to him.

She'd gone to each of them. She'd kissed and hugged them and tucked them all into bed. Even at fifteen Eduardo hadn't protested.

With the house quiet, Madeline closed the door to her bathroom and locked it. She ran the bathtub as full and as hot as she could. Then she took the pamphlets she'd received from the doctor's office out of her bag. As she sank into the hot bath with bubbles and candles surrounding her, she read about the cancer that was eating away at her body.

Her doctor had told her that her chances for survival were almost one hundred percent. But it was the word almost that had her nervous. She'd supported breast cancer research with donations and by walking in charity events. She'd even known a handful of women who had gone through it, including her boss. Never in a million years did she imagine she'd be going through it. Worse yet, she was going through it alone.

There was no reason to alarm her children. Until she had to, she'd keep it from them. Matt was gone. The end of her marriage only needed finalization from the courts. He'd even told her he was planning to take a job in Kentucky to put some distance between them. So certainly, she wasn't going to call him and tell him.

Madeline closed her eyes and began to sob.

The one person she knew she'd be able to count on would have been Carlos. But then she recalled all of the stories her

15

children had come home with. Each and every one of them had Kathy's name attached to it. He'd moved on. It was only a matter of time before Carlos found happiness and remarried. It had always surprised her he'd stayed single for so long.

He'd take care of the children if he had to. They seemed to like Kathy a lot. Perhaps she'd be a good mother to them if she...

She didn't want to think about Matt, cancer, or Carlos anymore. She dropped the pamphlets on the floor next to the tub and dropped her head under the water, waiting till her lungs burned with the need for oxygen before she came back up. It didn't help clear her thoughts of Carlos.

CHAPTER 4

*C*arlos watched Kathy set the table for dinner. She fit right in with the domestic lifestyle, he thought. She smiled when she caught his glance. "How is your sister?"

"Happier than I've ever seen her." He pulled a slice of carrot from the salad bowl and bit it in half. "Tyler is the love of her life."

She filled their glasses with the red wine he'd brought. "I never thought anyone would edge out Zach."

Carlos watched her as she moved the rest of the meal to the tiny table where he sat. She was so different from his ex-wife, Madeline. Thick blonde hair skimmed her shoulders. Her eyes were crystal blue and her figure was slim, fit, tall, and leggy. She was what every man had dreamed of when he was younger.

Madeline, on the other hand, was curvy and barely cleared five-foot-three. Her hair had been long when they'd fallen in love, but after each child was born, it got a little shorter. He liked the way she wore it now. It was a classic bob, as his daughter told him once. Madeline's eyes were as dark and rich as his were. She was full-blooded Italian and he was Puerto Rican. It had made for a beautiful mix in their children.

Kathy touched his arm and he looked up into her worried eyes. "You seem preoccupied. Are you okay?"

"I'm fine. I already miss the kids."

"You're a great father." She dipped her head down and brushed his lips with a gentle kiss. "Now what's really wrong? This isn't your usual I-miss-my-kids look."

They'd been together for almost six months, but in that time, she'd learned to read him. He couldn't hide anything from her. "Madeline was there."

"How is she?" She set the casserole dish on the table and then sat in her chair.

Carlos kept his eyes on her. She really was something. There wasn't even a hint of jealousy in her voice when she asked about Madeline's well being. That couldn't be normal, he thought. Wasn't the woman who came after the wife supposed to be bitter and hateful toward the ex?

He thought about seeing her. There had been worry in Madeline's eyes, which were shadowed with dark circles. The more he thought of it, her skin didn't glow as it normally did. "I don't think she's feeling very well. She set Tyler back in his bassinette and almost passed out."

Kathy's head snapped up. "Oh, no. What do you think is wrong? Did you call Curtis? Did he see her? If you think something is wrong, you should get her some help."

A smile crept across his lips.

Kathy's eyebrows rose. "Why are you smiling? People just don't pass out if they're healthy. You need to get her some help. Call Matt and see what's going on."

There was a warmth that spread though him as he watched Kathy study his reaction, while being genuinely concerned for his ex-wife.

"I love you." The words had flown from his mouth before he'd had time to consider them.

Kathy sat back in her chair and kept a cautious eye on him.

"Excuse me?"

"I love you," he repeated, and her eyes narrowed.

"I heard you, I just…"

"I know, I've never said it, but I'm saying it now." He reached for her hand and held it in his, keeping his eyes steady on hers. "You're amazing. You just sat here and completely worried about my ex-wife."

"Oh, Carlos." Kathy pulled her hand from his and stuck the spoon into the casserole. "She's a lovely woman. The two of you get along very well, and she's never been anything but nice to me. Why shouldn't I care about her?"

"Because she's my ex-wife."

"And the way you've always talked about her, I'm not sure why that is."

How many times had he heard that? The thought had him squirming in his seat. "Point is that's what she is. She's married to my ex-best friend, and they live in my ex-house."

She laughed. "And she's a very lucky woman to have you as a friend."

"Thank you."

"Now eat." She spooned casserole onto his plate, and he caught her arm. "What?"

"Move in with me." He felt her pulse rise under his fingertips. It wasn't anything they'd ever discussed, so he knew he'd caught her off guard.

"What's gotten into you?"

"I want us to be together."

She pulled her arm back. "We are together."

"You know what I mean. I love you. Does that mean anything to you?"

Kathy sat back and studied him.

He cocked his eyebrow "You'd better answer me or I just might ask you to marry me."

Her eyes widened and she let out a nervous laugh. "Okay,

okay! I'll move in with you."

"Good." He tugged her arm until she slid out of her chair and onto his lap. "We'll start with that," he said as he pressed his lips to hers and they became pliant and warm.

CHAPTER 5

*M*adeline walked from the doctor's office. Her knees were weak and her breast was sore where they had taken the biopsy. There was no option to walk all the way to the car before she broke down. She found a chair in the waiting room at the hospital and sat. Tears streamed down her face, and she tried to brush them away as they fell.

She'd undergo a double mastectomy in three weeks. She'd check in two days after Christmas and begin a rigorous treatment schedule of chemo. If she was lucky enough and the cancer was gone, she could have reconstructive surgery and have her breasts recreated. As it was, it was too much to think about.

The first thing she would do would be to ask Carlos to take the kids for a few extra weeks. Maybe she could tell him she'd be out of town. Until she knew if they could get the cancer, she didn't want anyone worrying about her, especially her kids. She was doing that enough for everyone. Her boss had been through this stupid thing called cancer, twice. She knew she could lean on her for the support she'd need.

Madeline thought of herself as a strong enough person to get through the surgery, and if the kids were with Carlos she'd have time to recover. Her parents could be there in case she needed them. But her plan was to keep it as far from her family as she could, until she absolutely had to tell them.

If there was an upside to divorce, it was that she could send the kids away, and have time to do this on her own.

Madeline waited until she was home and seated at the kitchen table with a glass of water and an icepack on her breast before she called Carlos. Breathing exercises she'd learned in yoga classes weren't doing much to calm her as she dialed his phone number.

"Hello," Kathy answered, and the discomfort in Madeline's chest increased, though it might have been heartbreak that caused it.

"Kathy? It's Madeline."

"Madeline! How are you? Carlos said you weren't feeling well before Thanksgiving. Are you feeling better?"

She swallowed hard and batted away more tears that tried to push their way through. She should have known he'd have been worried enough to say something to Kathy. Truth was, she was surprised she hadn't had a visit from his brother, Doctor Curtis.

"I'm doing much better. I must have been trying to catch something."

"I'm glad to hear it."

Madeline swallowed hard. "Is Carlos there?"

"He just went out to the truck to get a few more boxes."

"Boxes?"

"He asked me to move in." Kathy's voice rose in a delighted pitch. "We're unloading all my junk right now. I can't believe how much stuff I have. And neither can Curtis. He must have commented on it a thousand times while he was loading it for me."

Madeline forced a laugh. "Leave it to Curtis."

"Can I have him call you back?"

"Oh, I can catch him later. Congratulations on your new living arrangements," she choked on her own words.

"Thank you. I think he's thinking about getting married." Kathy's voice had dropped to almost a whisper.

Madeline gripped the phone tighter and squeezed her eyes closed. "I'm sure he is. He's a lucky man to have found you."

"That means the world coming from you," she said, and Madeline heard the voices of men in the background. "Oh, wait. Here he is. Madeline is on the phone for you," she heard Kathy say and then the obvious jumbling sound as the phone was passed off.

"Maddie?" he said, and she smiled. It had been a long time since he'd called her that, and she wasn't comfortable with how it still melted her inside. "What's up?"

"Oh, I didn't mean to bother you. I hear you're getting a new roommate."

"Yeah. About time, don't you think?"

"Uh-huh." A twist of nausea hit her stomach. "You know, I can talk to you later."

"No. What did you need?"

"Well..." She tried to keep her voice light and happy. "I'm taking a trip out of town. I was wondering if the kids could stay with you for about three weeks."

"Wow. That must be some trip." His voice lifted, and she knew he was happy for her. It broke her heart that it was all a lie. "Early Christmas present from Matt?"

"Just a trip." The weight of her deception was heavy in her chest. She'd never lied to Carlos in all the years she'd known him. It wasn't easy to do.

"Sure. That won't be any problem."

"Great. I really appreciate it."

"Sure. Oh, Maddie, don't say anything to the kids yet about Kathy moving in. I want to surprise them."

She cleared her throat. They were going to have a lot of surprises. "Okay. Thanks, Carlos."

She disconnected the call and put her head between her knees. Kathy had moved in. She knew Carlos well enough. They'd be married in six months.

~

CHRISTIAN PUSHED AROUND THE CEREAL IN HIS BOWL. "YOU REALLY have to go for three weeks?"

Madeline watched him as he tried to act uninterested, but that wasn't Christian. His heart was always on his sleeve. "You'll be with your dad and Kathy. You'll be fine."

He only nodded his head.

Clara smeared jelly on her toast. "He said I can hold Tyler on Saturday. Aunt Regan and Uncle Zach are going out to dinner, and we're watching him."

"You be careful with him," Madeline warned.

"I will be."

Eduardo shuffled through the kitchen.

"Well good morning, sunshine. Glad you could join us." She turned to kiss his cheek.

His eyes shot open, and he took a step back. "Wow, Mom! Are you okay?"

"Yeah, I'm fine."

"You're burning up." He put the back of his hand to her head as if she were a child. "Maybe you'd better go back to bed."

"I'll lie down when you all get on the bus." She forced a smile through the sickness that was taking over her body. "Do you have your presents for your teachers? It's the last day before break. There isn't a second chance to get them to them before Christmas."

"Yeah, Mom." Eduardo nodded, his eyes still focused on her and filled with worry. "Why don't you call Matt and see if he can come over and take care of you while I'm at school. He could at least do that much for you."

She was sure that if a breaking heart could make a sound, they'd have heard it. She forced a smile to her lips to ward off his worry. "I'll be fine. I have the day off. I can rest. Sit down and eat your breakfast."

Cancer had turned her into a liar. Every day she waited for her nose to start growing like Pinocchio's. She'd even called her parents and asked them to fly to Nashville so she could have a routine surgery. When her mother had asked what routine meant, Madeline told her she was having a growth removed. The lie had some merit—she didn't want to upset her parents. Her mother had agreed, but then had gone on talking about the vacation they wanted to take, and that visiting her would mean that would have to wait. Madeline needed them there, so she couldn't let her mother's comments bother her.

Madeline only hoped they'd get there in time to help her.

CHAPTER 6

*C*hristmas was a blur. She and Carlos had shared their time with the kids between Christmas Eve and Christmas morning. With gifts and an abundance of food, Madeline wasn't sure the kids even cared anymore about not seeing her for three weeks.

The morning after Christmas, she took the kids to Carlos' house and waited in the driveway for them to get all of their things from the car.

Carlos appeared at the back door and waved. She plastered on another fake smile and waved back. "I think they brought the whole house."

"We'll try to keep track of it all," he laughed as Clara walked toward him. "Do you have time for a cup of coffee?"

That was so Carlos. He was her best friend in the world, and she couldn't tell him what she was going through. Her skin chilled under her heavy coat. "No. I have to finish packing."

"Send us a postcard."

She nodded, kissed her kids good-bye, and drove away in tears.

. . .

MADELINE'S PARENTS HADN'T MADE THEIR FLIGHT, AND SHE'D BEEN forced to call her boss and ask for the biggest favor any employee could request. She needed a ride to the hospital at four the next morning and would have to have her there until she was wheeled into surgery. By then her parents should be there and everything would work out, or so she hoped.

Madeline's boss, Sylvia, was an expert with all the paperwork and helped her understand what it was she was signing. She was also an expert on the process and she did everything she could to keep Madeline calm, but it wasn't working very well.

The check-in process took an hour, then they escorted her to a room. As the sun came up, the nurses prepped Madeline for surgery. In a few hours they would go in and remove the cancer along with her breasts. Swallowing hard, she tried to relax. As long as she was able to remain on the Earth and have her children, she didn't care what she looked like.

DR. CURTIS KELLER SLUNG HIS COMMUTER BAG OVER HIS SHOULDER and rubbed his eyes. He'd been at the hospital for thirty-six hours. It was time to go home and crawl into bed for the next three days. He stepped back from the elevator to let the nurses push the gurney toward surgery and then he stepped into the elevator, only to step back off.

He watched as they pushed the gurney through the doors to surgery and he turned back toward the desk. There on the wall was the surgery schedule for the day. M. CARSON was written under Dr. Martin.

"Samantha." He leaned on the desk and gave a slow wink to the nurse who sat in front of a computer. "Hey, what's Martin got going on this morning?"

Knowing she could get in trouble, she rolled her chair closer to him and leaned in. "Mastectomy."

"Shit," he whispered. "Mr. Carson? Is he in the waiting room?"

She shrugged. "I don't think there's anyone here. A woman was with her when they checked in and said that Ms. Carson's parents should arrive before she's out of surgery." She held up a finger and rolled back to the computer. With a few keystrokes, she opened the file and quickly closed it. "Mr. Carson is not listed on her paperwork. Next of kin is listed as Carlos Keller." She knit her brows together. "Relative of yours?"

"You certainly could say that." He reached out and touched her arm. "Hey, I owe you one. Dinner this week?"

"Can't. Catch me next week."

"Deal." He turned toward the waiting room.

Matt Carson wasn't anywhere. Curtis shook his head and pulled out his cell phone. The family waiting area was one of the only places his cell phone was allowed.

The phone rang in his ear and before his brother could even mutter the word hello, he was firing off questions. "Carlos, hey, where's Madeline?"

"What? She's out of town for a few weeks. The kids are staying with me."

He gave a cluck with his tongue and shook his head. He'd known Madeline as long as Carlos had, and he knew what she was doing. She didn't want anyone worrying about her, but she'd once married into the wrong family for that. "Can you get down here to the hospital?"

"Okay, bro, you're freaking me out. What the hell is going on?"

Curtis rubbed the tension out of his neck then scrubbed his hand over his face. "Listen, I don't want to freak you out, but..." He blew out a breath. "Madeline was just wheeled into surgery."

CHAPTER 7

*C*urtis was right where Carlos expected to find him. He sat in the corner of the family waiting room, his head propped up against the wall, his arms folded across his chest. He was sound asleep.

Carlos nudged his arm and Curtis jolted up in the chair and batted his eyes.

"Hey," Curtis groaned as he tried to wake up.

"Now tell me what the hell is going on. I ran out of the damn house. I made Kathy call into work and tell them she had some emergency, and all of this was done without the kids hearing any of it. Now I'm freaking the hell out and so is Kathy."

"Shut up for two damn minutes and sit down." His brother rubbed his hands over his eyes and sat up in the chair as Carlos took the seat next to him. "I happened to pass them as they were taking her into surgery. I didn't know she was here, did you?"

"I told you. She said she was going out of town."

Curtis nodded. "She checked in this morning. She's scheduled for a double mastectomy."

Carlos chewed on his bottom lip and inched in closer to his

brother. "You're going to pretend like I'm really, really dumb. What the hell does that mean?"

"She has breast cancer, Carlos."

Carlos felt the blood drain from his face and he knew his brother had seen it, because he jerked Carlos' shoulders and shoved his head down between his knees. His stomach knotted and he felt like Curtis had just punched him right in the gut.

When he could, he sat up. Curtis stood before him with a cup of water.

"Drink."

He did as his brother told him. After looking around the waiting room, he looked up at Curtis.

Curtis shook his head as if he'd read his mind. "Matt's not here."

"Why the hell not? If your wife is going through this, you're here!"

"He's not listed on any of her paperwork. She's listed as single, and you're listed as the emergency contact and next of kin."

His mouth fell open. "What's going on?"

"I don't know." Curtis rubbed the back of his neck with his hand then fell into the chair next to Carlos. "I checked with the nurse, and it'll be a few hours before she's out of surgery. I'm going to see to it that you can be there when she wakes up."

Carlos nodded. That was right where he wanted to be.

"Do you have any way to get in touch with Matt?" Curtis asked.

Carlos shrugged. "I'll call Kathy and ask her to look in my contacts on my computer. Maybe Eduardo knows."

"Okay. Let me go see if there's any news."

Carlos sat in the waiting room, surrounded by family members of other patients. He felt sick. Every part of him hurt, especially his heart.

When he was calm enough he called home, and Kathy

answered the phone on the first ring. "Sweetheart, what happened? Is she okay? Was there an accident?"

"I'll let you know all about it when I get home."

"I can come down."

"No. I need you to be calm and just be with the kids." He swallowed the lump in his throat that had formed when he thought about the kids finding out their mother was sick.

"Okay." He heard her take a deep breath.

"I need you to look in the contacts on my computer. I need to find Matt Carson's phone number."

Sounds from the keyboard filtered through the phone. He looked at the small table next to him and noticed there were a notepad and a hospital pen laid out for those who waited here, unprepared in more ways than just lacking writing implements.

He heard Eduardo's voice in the room with Kathy. "What are you looking for?"

"Matt's phone number," he heard her say, and Carlos shook his head.

"He moved out," Eduardo said, loud and clear.

"Kathy, let me talk to Ed." He heard the phone pass hands. "What do you mean he moved out?"

"They're getting a divorce. He moved out before Thanksgiving. She didn't tell you?"

"No." Carlos took a deep breath. "Neither did you."

"I guess I figured she would have told you. She tells you everything."

Evidently, she was keeping a lot of secrets lately.

"Let me talk to Kathy again," he said, and the phone changed hands. "I'll fill you in when I get home and I have more answers. She's fine, and I don't want the kids to know until I tell them."

"Okay." He heard the lift in her voice. He could trust her to keep quiet until he could talk to his children.

. . .

CARLOS DRANK THREE CUPS OF COFFEE AND PACED THE FLOOR while Curtis slept in the corner of the waiting room. He'd told him to go home, but Curtis wouldn't move. He was stubborn, and Carlos was happy to have him there. He needed his brother.

When the nurse entered the room and began to speak to Carlos, Curtis shot right up. "They've moved her to recovery. As soon as she's stable, you can go back and sit with her," the nurse said, and Carlos nodded.

"Thank you." His mouth was dry. The room was still spinning, and all he could think about was gathering Madeline up in his arms and holding her tight.

Guilt washed over him.

He'd professed his love to Kathy and moved her into his house. When would he stop thinking of Madeline as his wife and feeling as if he needed to take care of her every moment?

CHAPTER 8

The color was returning to her skin, and the monitor that read her vital signs began to beep a little faster.

Carlos watched her carefully as her eyelids began to flutter. A few moments later, she fully woke up and turned to him. He'd been sitting by her side for over an hour, whispering words of encouragement in her ear. Now he kissed her cheek.

"You did great." He smiled.

"What... are you"—she tried to swallow—"doing here?"

"Did you think anything would escape a Keller?" He brushed her cheek with his fingers. "Curtis saw you being wheeled into surgery and called me."

"I'm sorry. I didn't..."

"Shhh. Don't talk now. We'll have time for that."

Madeline nodded and her eyes drifted closed.

He'd gone down to the cafeteria to get some food when they'd moved her to a room.

A smile crossed her lips when he entered and he knew she appreciated his being there.

"The doctor says the surgery went well." Her words were now

fluid and he could tell she was feeling better. Her eyes were glassy from the pain medication, but her smile was genuine.

"Good."

"Thank you for being here. I didn't think it would matter to have someone there when I woke up, but it did."

"You should have asked me to be here." He pulled a chair close to her bedside and leaned into her. Careful not to disturb the wires and tubes attached to her. He eased his hand into hers. "Do you want to tell me why I think you're on a vacation?" He raised his eyebrows.

Madeline diverted her gaze out the window. "I was scared. I didn't want anyone to know what was going on until it was over. You're kind of a worrywart," she said, turning her misty eyes back to his.

"You're kind of important to me." And that was an understatement.

"That means a lot to me."

"Now"—he set his jaw and leaned in closer—"when did Matt leave?"

She took a deep breath and shook her head. "He's been gone for a month. We're just waiting for the finalization of the divorce papers. We split amicably, so it shouldn't take too long."

Carlos shook his head. He'd thought he was angry when they got married, but it wasn't even comparable to how he felt now, knowing that Matt had let her down. "Maddie, I'm so sorry."

She shook her head again. "Don't be. I'm okay with it." Her brow furrowed and she turned her head directly toward him. "You shouldn't be here. You should be home with Kathy."

"Kathy knows where I am. She's worried about you." He reached his free hand to her face and brushed a strand of hair away from her eyes. "I'm going to be here until they kick me out and then I'll be back in the morning."

"Don't be ridiculous. You need to be home with the kids and Kathy."

"You don't get it, do you?" Carlos stood and walked toward the window. He looked out over the other buildings on the campus and thought of all the people who lay in the beds with someone who loved them by their sides. "You're very important to me. Jesus, Maddie, we have a life together, still. What would have happened if this didn't go well? I'd get some mysterious call that..." He couldn't say it. "Damnit, does Matt even know?"

Madeline shook her head. Tears were falling from her eyes.

Carlos pulled a tissue from the box on the table next to her and wiped away the tears.

"Don't you think he'd want to know? You're selling yourself short thinking that none of us matter."

"I just didn't want anyone to worry."

"Well, it didn't work. Getting a call from my brother telling me he just passed you being wheeled into surgery was a bit of a shock this morning."

"I'm sorry," she said again. Her eyes then flew open wide. "The kids?"

"They don't know a thing yet. But they sure as hell will when I get home. You can't keep this from them. They have a right to know."

She nodded. "I'm so sorry."

"Will you stop it?" He sat back down and took her hand. "You're not alone and you're not going to be. I'm here for you. I'll always be here for you."

"But Kathy..."

"Knows how I feel about you." Of course he'd downplayed that quite a bit. He still felt very deeply for Madeline, and it ripped at his heart when he thought about having told Kathy he loved her. "She'll be here for you too."

. . .

CARLOS LEFT MADELINE'S SIDE AROUND DINNERTIME. THE DRIVE home gave him plenty of time to think about what he was going to tell them.

He wished he didn't have to. God, how he wished she were on a three-week vacation with her husband.

Dinner had been cleared by the time he opened the door and walked into the house. The kids were putting away the last of the condiments and wiping down the table. Kathy stood at the counter, a cup of tea in her hand as she watched him walk through the door.

"Hey guys." He forced a smile to his lips, but he didn't feel it in his heart.

"Hey, Dad. Where have you been?" Eduardo, the most observant, was the first to ask.

Carlos took a deep breath and set his keys on the counter. He kissed Kathy gently on the lips and gave her a look to say thank you and then he turned to his children. All eyes were now on him. All movement had stopped. He pulled a chair out from the table and sat down. He nodded to Kathy to do the same, and the kids followed suit.

"Before I even begin this conversation with you, I want to start by saying everything is okay." He made eye contact with all of them. "Do you understand?" Three sets of dark eyes kept on him as they nodded.

"Your mom isn't on vacation. She had surgery today and she didn't want you to worry about her."

"She's sick, isn't she?" Eduardo slapped his hands down on the table. "She's run-down and the other day she had a fever. She's really, really sick, huh?"

Carlos placed his hand atop Eduardo's and nodded. "She's very, very sick." He saw Clara's eyes begin to pool and soon the tears had fallen. He reached for her and she climbed up on his lap. "She doesn't want you to worry about her, and she'd be sad if she knew you were."

"What's wrong with her?" The question came from Christian, who usually sat quietly.

Again, Carlos took a deep breath. "Your mom has breast cancer."

"Oh, God!" Eduardo's eyes filled with tears.

Christian pushed from the table and went to his room. He'd go to him after he explained the situation to the others. It was just how Christian dealt with things.

"Listen, that's why she had surgery. Hopefully, they got all of the cancer and she'll be fine. She'll have another procedure in a few days to take out some tubes they had to leave in there. She'll have to go through chemo, and then she'll have some reconstruction done."

Kathy lifted her hand to her chest and batted away tears he saw lingering in her eyes. He looked at Clara. Her face was creased with confusion. Eduardo's face, on the other hand, was set in anger. He understood that. He was angry with Madeline for not telling him the truth. He was mad at Matt for leaving her. And he was pissed off at the cancer for attacking the woman he loved.

"But for now she's in the hospital and they're keeping a close eye on her."

"Why wouldn't she tell us? That's not fair. She can't do this to us." Eduardo shook his head squeezed his hands into fists, popping his knuckles as he did so.

"She's scared. She found out she had cancer the day after Matt left. She feels that if you knew she's sick you'd treat her differently. All she wants to do is take care of you. But now she needs us to take care of her. We're all going to help her through this."

Kathy nodded. "Your dad is right. We're all going to help her."

Carlos smiled through his pain. "Thank you. You sure are amazing."

"I want to see her," Clara whispered against his chest.

39

"You will. We're going down there to see her tomorrow. She's going to be mad as hell at me for it, but I don't really care. She needs you, and once you're there, she'll understand. I'm going to go call Grandma and Grandpa too. They were supposed to be here, but their flight was delayed until tomorrow." He kissed the top of Clara's head. "Now I have to find Matt." He really needed to know what's going on, even if he didn't come to be with her—and that thought had Carlos' blood boiling.

"Mommy's really lucky you still love her so much," Clara said. Carlos knew she didn't mean any harm in her comment, but his eyes darted toward Kathy's and he saw the flash of pain.

CHAPTER 9

*C*arlos peeked around the door and watched Madeline as she shifted to see him. He'd expected her to look better, but her skin was pale, her eyes sunken and dark. His stomach knotted. "Good morning, beautiful. How are you feeling?"

"Like I was run over by a truck," she said softly as tears filled her eyes.

He walked to the side of the bed and gathered her hand in his. "What's wrong?"

"I'm scared. I'm so scared."

"Oh, baby." He pressed a kiss to her forehead. "You need to think positive. What you went through yesterday was enormous. One step at a time."

She nodded and took a deep breath. "What are you doing here?"

"I told you I was going to come back and take care of you."

"I'm not your responsibility anymore."

"Yes, you are. You're very important to me," he said, and that pang of guilt was back. The look in Kathy's eyes when Clara had said he still loved Madeline flashed in his mind. But he knew Kathy understood. "I have a surprise for you."

"For me?"

"Are you up for it?"

She nodded.

"Okay, I'll be right back."

A moment later, he returned with Eduardo, Clara, and Christian. Each of them held a long-stemmed rose.

Her eyes opened wide and weak smile settled on her lips. "Oh, my babies." She began to sob, and Christian stopped his progression into the room, but Carlos pulled him in.

Eduardo advanced toward her first and kissed her. "Hey, Mom. You doing okay?"

"Yeah. I'm doing okay." She smiled and moved her hand to grasp his.

"Why didn't you tell us? You should have told us."

"I know. I just didn't want you to worry about me."

His lips thinned and he looked away, and then back at her. "I was already worried about you. I knew you were sick."

Clara couldn't speak through her tears. She walked to her mother and rested her head on the pillow next to her, and Madeline nuzzled against her with her cheek. "It's okay, baby. I'm okay."

Christian kept his distance, but he smiled when she looked at him.

Carlos knew they had their ways of dealing with things. He excused himself and stood outside of the room. There was a long road ahead of them. He had to decide how to deal with the fact that they needed each other, but he also needed to distance himself. There was no way he'd let her be alone. Damnit, it hadn't been a lie. He needed her. She was an intrinsic part of his life. But now he had Kathy and he had to watch his step.

He'd lost sleep over seeing the pain caused when Clara said he loved Madeline. Who wouldn't be pissed by something like that? Worse yet, he hadn't—couldn't have—corrected her. He'd never stopped loving Madeline.

There had always been that small part of him that secretly wished for Matt to leave so he could reclaim his wife. Who'd have thought the opportunity would arise the moment he fell in love with someone else?

He pulled the slip of paper from his pocket, took out his phone, and dialed the number he'd scribbled on the paper. There were still enough connections to Matt Carson, and he'd known who to ask.

"Matt, it's Carlos." Irritation filtered through his voice, but there was no way to hide it as he told the man who'd once been his best friend that the woman they'd both loved had cancer.

CARLOS RETURNED TO THE HOSPITAL LATER THAT EVENING AFTER taking the kids home and feeding them dinner. Kathy was edgy and he couldn't blame her. She was being a great sport, and he'd make it up to her.

When Madeline was healthy and home, he figured he'd ask Kathy to marry him. After all, he'd made the phone call to Matt Carson himself. The man was already in the car and heading back to Nashville before he'd hung up to take care of his wife. Carlos wouldn't stand in the way.

He scrubbed his hands over his face. The heavy stubble on his cheek reminded him he'd forgotten to shave that morning. He'd been in such a hurry to get to Madeline's side.

Carlos tapped on Madeline's door and she invited him in. This time she looked happy, and the glow had returned to her skin. She looked stiff sitting in her bed, and he knew the bandages wrapped around her made her uncomfortable. There would be time to deal with that, he thought. She'd be upset the first time they let her see what they'd done to her.

"You look better."

"I feel better. I hate you for bringing the kids, but thanks. That really helped me out."

He leaned in and kissed her cheek. "I know you pretty well."

"Did my parents ever get on the plane?"

He laughed as he pulled the chair to her bedside. "Yes, they finally got a flight. They'll be here soon." He took her hand and absentmindedly kissed her fingers.

Madeline nodded. "I owe you. This was bigger than me. I was afraid I was going to die. I couldn't handle it."

"You're going to be fine and I'll be here for you."

"No, you won't."

His head snapped up.

Madeline lowered her hand slowly to the bed. "You've started a new life. You really need to focus on Kathy and building a life together. I'm just in your way."

"I don't think it matters right now. Right now I'm focused on seeing you through this."

"Well, I don't want you to. Mom and Dad will take care of me."

"So you're just dismissing me?"

Her eyes shifted away from him. "Yes."

"It's not important to you to have me here?"

"I appreciate it. I've thanked you. Now I think you should go. They're sending me home soon. Trust me. You'll just be in the way when my mom gets here."

He stood and raked his fingers through his hair. "I can't believe you. I can't believe you'd just push me to the side. I want to take care of you."

"Carlos, I'm not yours to take care of."

He could feel his heart being squeezed by her words, and his body temperature began to rise as his anger surfaced. "And whose fault is that?"

"Excuse me?"

"Nothing," he said throwing his hands in the air. "Nothing."

"Listen, we ended this five years ago. Move on."

"That's what you want?"

"Yes."

"Fine. Tell your parents I'll bring the kids anytime." Carlos turned and walked out of the room with his hands balled into fists by his sides. If he were anywhere but the damn hospital, he'd put his fist through the wall. How dare she dismiss him like that? When you loved someone you wanted to take care of them.

He stopped in the middle of the hall and let the thought wash over him.

Of course he loved her. They shared a family. But she was right. She wasn't his to worry about anymore. The thought made him sick, but he walked out of the hospital knowing this was what she wanted, no matter how wrong he thought she was.

As soon as the door closed, Madeline let lose the flood of tears that she'd been holding back. That had been the hardest thing she'd done since the day they both decided separating was best for them. She sank down in her bed and sobbed.

Her heart was breaking, and that hurt worse than the throbbing in her chest from her stitches and bandages. She loved him. She loved him so much. How could she hurt him by tearing him from the woman he now loved? He'd hate her for it if Kathy ever left. She'd done the right thing. No matter how much it hurt her, she had to make sure he moved on.

"Madeline?"

She turned as the door opened and Matt walked through. The pain that rolled in her stomach from telling Carlos to leave had balled into a solid mass of anger when she saw Matt's face. She didn't want him there, and someone had told him what had happened.

Kathy poured herself a cup of coffee and watched as Carlos dragged himself into the kitchen and sat down at the table. She let out a slow and steady breath. Did he think she didn't notice that he'd crawled out of bed, taken a shower in the middle of the night, and spent the rest of the night on the couch? She set her mug on the table and sat down next to him. "I left some pamphlets on your desk. Did you find them?"

"Pamphlets? No." He picked up the newspaper she'd laid there to read and began to thumb through it.

"They were wedding packages. There are some nice places that we can do the ceremony and the reception. I was also thinking, that maybe, Regan and Zach would let us have the wedding out at their place. With all the beautiful land, we could even have a tent put up out back by her rose gardens."

"Sure," he said looking up at her finally. "I'm going to go buy Eduardo a phone."

"Okay." Her voice dipped. Had he not heard her at all?

"They'll be going to Madeline's tomorrow night, and I thought that this way he could call me and keep up with me."

"He can't just call from her phone at the house?"

"Oh, you know. If she needs me. If he needs me." He looked back down at the ad in the newspaper for a wireless phone store.

Kathy set her jaw. She had to remind herself that Carlos was the kind of man who would take care of the mother of his children. He was also the kind of man who would do that with all of his heart. The only problem was, as the woman he'd supposedly given his heart to, she was becoming to find it hard to accept his generosity.

She sipped at her coffee as she watched him. There was a high road, and she was going to take it. He'd asked her to marry him and he wouldn't have done that if he hadn't wanted to. Planning for the wedding would continue. She'd involve him only as much as he wanted to be involved, but she wanted a nice wedding. Madeline would be welcomed of course, but she certainly hoped in the few months that it would take them to plan the event, Madeline's illness would take a backseat.

She stood and walked to the sink to rinse out her mug. The coffee was bitter on her tongue and her attitude was bitter in her heart. She wasn't used to being jealous and she didn't like it one bit. "I'm heading into the office. When can I expect you?"

"I'll be home right after school to get the kids. Then I'll take them over to Maddie's."

Kathy winced at the pet name.

"We can go out for dinner," he offered, finally looking up at her.

"Fine." She left without kissing him good-bye.

THE PHONE HE'D PICKED OUT WAS BASIC, BUT IT WOULD BE USEFUL. He handed it to Eduardo, whose eyes grew wide. "The phone isn't for socializing or texting. It's just for you and me to keep in contact. Understand?"

"Got it."

"Before your first class every day, I want you to call me and tell me how she is."

Eduardo looked over the phone he'd handed him. "Dad, why don't you just call her yourself?"

"She doesn't want me looking after her."

"That's ridiculous." Eduardo looked up at him. "You've always taken care of her. Even when Matt was here."

"I know, but she was specific." He placed a hand on Eduardo's shoulder. "She's willing to let you be here and take care of her. I think that's going to help her out."

"I hope so." His son looked up at him and gave him a crooked smile.

"Me too."

He'd dropped the kids off and stood in the street in front of the house he and Madeline used to share. She hadn't come to the door as she usually would, and that was weighing on his mind.

. . .

47

KATHY HAD FOUR MORE PAMPHLETS FOR WEDDING LOCATIONS, AND before Carlos knew it, Regan, Zach, and Tyler had joined them for dinner upon invitation from Kathy.

His head was spinning with wedding talk and plans. Regan was as bad as Kathy. He sat quietly, too deep in his own thoughts to care about the conversation around him.

Zach held little Tyler against his shoulder and patted his back. "Damn, Monday-night football. How did I let you convince me to leave the house?" Zach kissed his son and handed him to his wife. "Carlos, let's leave these lovely ladies to discuss bridal bouquets and run into the bar and check out the game."

Carlos' head snapped up at the offer. Regan patted Tyler on the back and nodded. Kathy kept making notes in her bridal planner. He wasn't sure she was aware he was leaving the table.

Zach slapped him on the shoulder as they turned the corner into the bar. "You were looking lost, my friend. I think you could use a beer and a few moments of man time."

"Yeah, thanks."

Zach ordered them each a beer and then turned to the big-screen TV. The crowd in the upscale bar hooted and hollered as the Titans scored another touchdown.

"That's what I'm talking about!" Zach hollered too. "You didn't even see that."

"What? Sorry."

"What's got your head so full?" Zach took a pull from his beer.

"I'm waiting to hear from Ed. I figured he'd call and tell me how Maddie was doing."

"You do know you're not married to her anymore, right?"

"I know. I'm worried about her. Matt left her. Her folks went back to California. I just don't think she should be alone right now."

"She's not. She has her children." Zach nudged him. "What are you doing marrying Kathy?" His voice was hushed, and Carlos looked up at him.

"I love her."

Zach shook his head. "I don't doubt that. But you love Madeline too."

"I've always loved Maddie. I've loved her since I was fifteen."

"Do you hear yourself?" Zach saw a table open up and he grabbed their bottles and guided Carlos toward it. "Matt's gone. Madeline is sick, and you can't keep her off your mind for ten minutes to help your new fiancée plan your wedding. Don't you see what's going on here?"

He rubbed the pain of regret from his chest. "I care about her."

"And you always have. Hell, I remember the night I met you and she dropped the kids off at your folks' house. You were crushed and your father was angry because you'd been divorced for two years, and yet you still mourned your marriage. In the three years I've known you, I've never known you to even try to move on from Madeline. Now she's single and you've chosen this time to get married."

Carlos rolled the bottle between his palms and looked down at it. "She doesn't want me in her life. She'd rather have me gone and happy."

"But you're not."

Carlos sat silent for a moment. "No, I'm not."

"Did you ever think she was trying to push you away in case something happened to her? She'd rather have you angry at her than mourn her."

There were tears stinging Carlos' eyes, but he fought them back and took a swig from his beer.

Zach inched further over the table. "Listen, Regan did the same thing. Remember Michael Hamilton?"

"You don't forget the name of the man who tried to kill your sister."

"Once she realized he was the man I was doing business with, she quit her job and planned to move away so she wouldn't hurt me with her past. She figured I was better off without her." He shook his head. "What if I would've let her go? What if I would've let that asshole's money mean more than my love for Regan? I wouldn't have anything right now. But look, we've been happily married for three years and we have a son. You know how that feels."

He did. There was nothing like his children. The children he and Madeline had created in love were his life. "I just don't understand why she won't let me help her."

"She's scared."

Carlos inched his body over the table. "That's why she should let me help her."

"But she doesn't want you unhappy either. She thinks Kathy makes you happy."

"She does. Kathy is wonderful." The statement was as true as they came.

"I didn't say she wasn't. But does she really make you happy?

"Of course she does."

"As happy as Madeline makes you?"

Carlos rolled the beer bottle between his hands again and then pushed it away. "If you're trying to confuse, me you're doing a great job."

"No, I'm trying to get you to face something before you make a mistake." He finished his beer. "Listen. You need to do what you think is right. And what you think is right is to take care of Madeline."

"You think I should just butt into her life?"

"Yeah, I guess that's what I'm trying to say. But I also think you'd better give some consideration as to what you're going to do with Kathy. Do you really want to marry her? And if you really do, you need to either let go of your feelings for Madeline or make sure Kathy understands them completely. Because no matter how understanding she's being right now, sooner or later she's going to crack."

Carlos nodded.

"We'd better get back out there. Tyler is going to be getting hungry soon, and she'll want to head home to feed him."

Kathy was just closing her bridal planner when Zach and Carlos returned. Tyler slept peacefully in his carrier. Carlos watched as his sister's eyes rose toward her husband and he smiled at her. She returned the smile, and he knew in that silent moment they'd had an entire conversation.

Kathy looked up at Carlos. "I think I've decided on the outdoor wedding at Regan and Zach's. What do you think?"

"I think that sounds beautiful." He smiled. How could he not? She was absolutely glowing.

He sat back down next to her, and she scooted closer to him. "Do you like purple?"

"Purple is a fine color."

"Great. I think that Clara would look best in it. She's so beautiful." That warmed his heart. "I've asked my sisters to be bridesmaids, and your sisters too."

"Okay." He picked up the glass of water that he'd left there when he and Zach had vacated the table and sipped. "Well, Zach, I guess I'd better ask. Will you stand up on my side?"

Zach gave him a slow nod. "You know I would."

Carlos nodded. He'd ask Curtis and his boys too.

In that one moment he could see himself moving on.

Carlos held Kathy's hand as he navigated the dark roads single-handed as he'd done thousands of times. She was full of wildly excited chatter.

"Regan found a picture of the most beautiful dresses for the bridesmaids. I think we'll get one for Clara that will match. I think it would be nice to have her be a junior bridesmaid instead of a flower girl. Isn't she too old to be a flower girl?" Carlos only shrugged with a grunt, and Kathy continued. "Regan said Audrey would be a wealth of knowledge when it comes to caterers. She uses them for everything."

"It sounds like you know exactly what you want." He glanced her way and gave her a smile.

"Every girl dreams of what she wants from the time she's little. Of course, I don't expect you to dress in a white suit with braided ropes over the shoulders."

"Prince Charming, eh?"

"Of course."

He certainly couldn't imagine being someone's Prince Charming, but he found it refreshing that perhaps Kathy thought he was. "What else did you always want?"

"Well…" She sighed, obviously giving it some thought. "When I was about twenty, one of my friends from college got married. They set free white doves."

"Doves? What ever happened to rice?"

"So you're more old-fashioned? Shoe polish on car windows and tin cans strung to the back of the car?"

"Oh, yeah." He laughed. "When I was little, though, I do remember going to a wedding with my parents in Puerto Rico." He focused on the road as Kathy gave his hand a squeeze. It wasn't often that he thought of his birth parents or their family home in Puerto Rico.

They'd brought him to the States when he was nearly six. They'd become part of the community they lived in quickly, thanks to the church they'd belonged to. That was where he met the Keller family for the first time. Regan was his age. The Kellers had adopted her and Arianna, her older sister, after having been their foster parents for years. He could still see Regan with ponytails in a white dress for church the first time he'd ever laid eyes on her. Mrs. Keller had a little boy in her arms, and he was sleeping. It was so vivid in his mind.

Emily Keller owned a small bakery with her parents. She'd given his mother work there. Alan Keller had helped to employ his father as a handyman. On that snowy December night, when his parents were killed, it was Emily Keller they called to the hospital to sit with him. By then, he was seven. The Kellers immediately took him in. Like Regan and Arianna, he never left.

The Kellers had only one child that they'd given birth to, and that was Curtis. But he was not favored or loved more than the three children that God had given them through other means.

Carlos gave Kathy's hand a squeeze back. He hadn't had to explain what he was thinking, she knew.

"What do you remember about that wedding?" she asked softly.

"I remember a plate of money. The priest would bless it and give it to the husband to give to the wife. Or something like that. And there was a doll." He shook his head. "I don't really remember why they had a doll dressed like the bride. First of all, it was a girl thing. Second, it was a little freaky." He laughed. "But it had charms on it, and they gave me one."

"Tradition?"

"I guess so. I was probably five, so I don't really remember it very well."

"Are most of your memories of you living with your mom and dad? I mean the Kellers?"

"Yeah. I had a grandmother in Puerto Rico, but I only remember her being old. She was too old to take care of me. So, when my parents died there wasn't the option of her taking me. She'd write to me, and my mom—Emily—would read them to me. But my grandmother died by the time I was nine."

She scooted closer to him so she could rest her head on his shoulder. "I love your parents. I'm very lucky to have them for future in-laws."

"I couldn't have gotten any luckier under the circumstances."

"What about Regan and Arianna. What about their birth parents?"

He gave a shrug of his other shoulder. "A young couple is all I know. The state took them away from them when Arianna was two and Regan was only a few months old. So Mom is really the only mom Regan has ever known, and Arianna doesn't remember her birth parents at all."

"Do you think Zach and Regan will have more kids?"

"Oh, yeah. At least one more. Regan knows the joy of having siblings." He shook his head with a laugh. "Okay, maybe not the joys, but we're a team. When one of us needs anything, the other ones are there. We all support Arianna's acting dreams. We all helped get Curtis though med school. When Regan lived in Hawaii with that guy"—he couldn't even say his name—"we supported her. And when she came back and needed support physically, mentally, and financially, we were there for her."

"So she would want Tyler to have that."

"I think so. And Zach sees the importance in it, having been an only child. He was shipped off to a boarding school in France."

Kathy lifted her head. "Zach speaks French?"

"Yup. It's funny too. You don't expect it, but when his friend Simone calls, it spews from his lips like it's his only language."

"Hmmm, I still have so much to learn about my new family."

Carlos gave a nod as she rested her head on his shoulder again. Family pulled together in times of trouble. There hadn't been a day since he was fifteen he didn't think of Madeline as family. Marrying Kathy wouldn't change that. He didn't expect it to. But how could he feel so far from Madeline now, and need her so much?

CHAPTER 10

*C*arlos drove around the block four times, trying to control his anger before he pulled into the driveway.

Damn her! He'd always wanted the best for her, and damnit, now he wanted to help her. Well, fine! He'd done what he could and that was all he could do.

He threw the car into park. *Damnit!* He hit the steering wheel and threw his head back against the seat. Why did it have to continue to be so hard?

Turning his head toward the house, he saw Kathy standing on the back step, watching him. She gave him a smile, but he assumed it was as forced as it looked. He blew out another breath. To hell with it. He was going to move on.

"Hey," was all he could think to say as he climbed out of the car.

She walked down the steps and into his arms. "Hey."

He held her there, taking in the comfort of her love. She tipped her head back and looked at him. "Is she doing better today?"

"Yeah, she's fine. Matt should be there now." He realized he hadn't told her Matt'd said he'd stop by. That would have

Madeline even more pissed at him. It wasn't his concern, he had to remember that. She was very clear about it.

"Her parents will be there in the morning. They'll take care of her."

"You did right calling Matt and taking the kids."

"I suppose." He gazed into her deep blue eyes. Her hair was pulled back, and it gave him the perfect view of her beautiful face. "Thank you for being so understanding. I don't think everyone in your position would have been."

"She's the mother of your children. I'd expect you to care."

Well, at least Kathy understood it even if Madeline didn't. "I love you," he said and swallowed hard past the lump in his throat.

"I love you too."

"I've been thinking." He pulled her in tighter. "Marry me."

She laughed a nervous laugh. "Wow, I didn't see that coming."

"I don't see any reason I should wait to ask. Will you marry me?" She didn't answer right away. Maybe his luck with the women in his life was in a bad way today. "You can think about it."

"I've done that a lot lately." Kathy wrapped her arms around his neck and pressed a warm, accepting kiss to his lips. "I would be honored to be your wife."

MADELINE HAD DRIFTED OFF TO SLEEP WHILE SHE WAS TALKING TO Matt. When she opened her eyes, he was still there. "I'm sorry. These pain medications make me so tired."

"No, it's okay." His voice cracked, and she knew he was nervous being in her presence. He never had dealt with crisis or illness well. It was why he'd decided to move to Kentucky. It was easier for him to run away from all of his problems than to stay and face them.

"I talked to your nurse. I was trying to see how things were going for you, but she said I wasn't on the list so she couldn't tell me anything."

"I'm sorry, again." She shook her head. She was the one in the hospital, so why was the one saying sorry all the time? "I didn't intend to tell you about the cancer. I didn't intend to tell anyone."

"Carlos called me."

Madeline nodded. She should have known he would. Wasn't it funny, as mad as she was at Matt for even standing there in front of her, she couldn't be mad at Carlos. He always did what he thought was right. "I should have figured he'd find you somehow."

"He told me Curtis caught you."

"Yeah, I hadn't even thought there'd be a chance he'd see me here."

He darted his eyes around the room, something he did when he couldn't bear to be around someone.

"How long will you be staying?" she asked, noting that the uneasy feeling between them was mutual.

He cleared his throat and gave a glance toward the door and back to her. "Oh, I can stay as long as you'd like me to."

"My parents are on their way, so really you don't need to uproot your life for me."

Again, he only nodded. The silence was suffocating her, and she knew he was as uncomfortable as she was. When he stood and paced the room with his hands in his pockets, she knew for a fact it would be the last time she'd see him. In his head he was working up one of his speeches—because Matt didn't make excuses. When he was ready to tell you what was on his mind, he did. "This might not be the time to do this, but I want to apologize for everything that happened between us."

There was a heaviness in her chest, the kind that came with years of regret. "Matt, I think since the day we decided to get married, we knew it wasn't going to be forever."

"Yeah." He ran his fingers through his hair. "You deserved

better than me. I never should have asked you to marry me. You were still in love with Carlos, and I ruined a twenty-year friendship with someone I considered my brother."

Damn the drugs. Tears were filling her eyes, and she shouldn't care at this point. She was lying there bandaged up because they were trying to save her life. "Are you sorry you married me?"

"No, I'm not sorry." He cleared his throat again. "It was great, while it lasted." Finally, he sat back down, and she adjusted to see him better. "It's just that I think when two people share their lives, they should love each other. I mean…" He was stumbling through his words. "What I want to say is… well… I did love you. I loved you like one of my best friends. You know?" She nodded. That's how she'd felt and she agreed. They should have been in love. "The hardest part was to know that you loved Carlos and you still do."

He was right again. It was always obvious that she loved Carlos more than she ever loved Matt. Acknowledging that only gave the pain she was feeling more depth as it drove into the pit of her stomach.

He stood again and paced. "God, this is killing me."

"Matt, what's going on?" She tried to sit up, but the bandages and wires held her in place.

"I shouldn't have come."

"Then why did you?" Her voice slipped into anger, and by the look in his eyes he'd noticed.

"I needed to make sure you were okay."

"I'm fine. I'll live. For now anyway."

He pursed his lips. "That's not funny."

"It's not supposed to be."

"I'm getting married." The words hit her like a fist in the stomach.

"Married?"

"Yeah. I didn't want to tell you like this…"

"My guess, Matthew, is that you didn't want to tell me at all."

The anger inside of her ramped up her heart rate. She heard the beeping on the machine speed up, and she took a deep breath.

"You should calm down."

"Go to hell. You've been gone one month. Did you move on so quickly? Did I mean so little?"

He shot a look at the door again. "I think I should go."

"I think you should be honest with me." The monitor to her side began beeping even faster, and she wondered if a nurse would burst through the door and make him leave, but no one came.

"You want me to be honest?" For the first time he made eye contact with her. "Fine." He stuffed his hands back into his pockets. "After Regan found out she was pregnant, you began pulling out pictures of you and Carlos and the kids. They were everywhere. You called him more often. You had lunch with him to discuss the kids. God, Madeline, it was like you had both of us on a string."

The deep breaths she'd been trying to take stuck in her lungs. She'd done that. She'd been that insensitive, and she didn't know it. "I'm sorry if I got sentimental."

"It's just that, well, I couldn't get a grip on it. I couldn't share in that joy with you. I didn't love you like he loved you." He sat back down and took her hand in his. "I strayed. God, it hurts to tell you that. I had an affair. I fell in love. I've never felt this way before."

Now she was holding her breath to stifle the anger. But tears that should have surfaced because her husband was telling he he'd fallen in love with someone else never came.

He looked away and then back at her. "She's pregnant and we're getting married and having a baby."

"Nice and tidy," she said through gritted teeth.

"Yeah, well just think, maybe you and Carlos can work things out. He's spent the last five years waiting for our marriage to fall apart so he could have you back."

"You are so stupid." She snapped out the words so fiercely that pain shot through her and had her biting back a scream. "Have you not listened to the kids for the last six months? He's in love with someone and she just moved in with him. They'll probably get married."

"Oh." He stood. "I guess I didn't realize…"

"You should have stayed in Kentucky."

"Listen, if there is anything I can do for you…"

"You can get the hell out of my room and go on with your life. Your community service here is done." She rolled away from him, wincing from the pain it caused, and didn't turn back until she heard the door close behind him.

CHAPTER 11

*M*adeline's parents were there when she woke the next morning. Her mother had been crying for two days straight and couldn't even look at her. How was she supposed to be of any help?

Her father sat in the corner of her room and just watched her mother fidget. These were the reasons she hadn't wanted to tell anyone about her surgery.

As the day crept into evening, the door had opened and her children had walked through. Finally, she thought, people who brought her real joy.

Each of them hugged her and then their grandparents. Even Christian had made it into the room and to her side before backing against a wall, neutral like her father.

She looked up into Eduardo's dark, sad eyes. "I didn't expect you."

"Dad wanted us to see you." Eduardo held her hand. "You look better."

"I'm feeling a little better. They'll take my drain tubes out, and I'll be out in a day or so."

"When you get home we want to stay with you. We've all discussed it. We want to help you though this."

"I think that would be wonderful." She patted her son's hand. "Where's your dad?"

Eduardo exchanged glances with Christian. "Kathy brought us."

"Oh." She was disappointed. She never should have been so nasty to him. "Kathy could have come in with you," she offered.

Eduardo ran his hand over the back of his neck. "I think she feels a little funny about that. I think she's wigging out now that they're getting married."

"Getting married?" The words croaked from her throat.

Eduardo exchanged glances with Christian again and then looked back at his mother. "I thought you knew."

She shook her head and swallowed the tears. "I'm happy for them." She smiled, but it almost hurt to do so.

Madeline's salvation came when the nurse announced that visitation was over.

Once the room was clear, she sobbed until she fell asleep.

MADELINE STOOD IN HER OWN BEDROOM, IN HER OWN BATHROBE, the front gaping open, and stared into the mirror. There were no tears. There were no words. She simply took in her mess that was now her chest.

There was nothing pretty left, not even a nipple. Her full C cups were gone, but she tried to remind herself that she'd spared her life by removing her breasts. How had it gotten so bad that she hadn't even known cancer was living in her body? How had she believed early detection was for everyone else? Not examining herself often enough had cost her both of her breasts.

She lay down on her own bed and pulled the blanket up to her chin. In the morning, she would welcome a brand-new year and would start her first round of chemo.

Madeline had done a lot of reading on it, and the side-effects were horrible. That seemed to be the way her life was going —horribly.

She'd need to get back to work the next week. No matter how much time she wanted to take to recover, physically ready or not, there were obligations. The thought of the medical bills that were beginning to add up had Madeline's head spinning. Worse, she knew there'd be more.

She turned scanned through her music playlist on her phone and selected the relaxing sounds of the ocean, and tried to will herself to relax and get some sleep. There was a lot to think about now that she was home. Her mother already had informed her that though they'd like to stay for months, her father, who had refused retirement, would need to get back to work.

The thought should have saddened her, but it didn't. As soon as they were gone, she could take charge of her life again.

Eduardo said he wanted to come home and help her, and of course that meant his brother and sister too. Madeline was seriously considering it. She'd convinced him to wait out the first week while her parents were there. The truth was, she wanted to see how the chemo would affect her. She didn't want to be sick in front of her kids.

As she lay alone in the dark, breathing in and out slowly, she thought about her fight with Matt. Who could have blamed him for what he'd done? They never did love each other the way she'd loved Carlos. They hadn't had sex in almost six months, and she didn't even care. Her marriage to Matt had been over long before he left.

It should have hurt, but hearing that Carlos and Kathy were engaged hurt even worse. She deserved that. Had she been totally honest about what was going on, maybe she wouldn't have turned away every man in her life.

She crossed her arms over her flat chest and tried to dull the pain. She didn't know if it was her stitches that hurt or her broken heart.

～

CARLOS LAY IN BED, KATHY WRAPPED IN HIS ARMS, WATCHING HER sleep. She was beautiful from the inside out. He knew he was a lucky man.

But even having her so close, he couldn't ease his mind. He wasn't thinking about the woman who had already started planning their wedding. He was thinking about Madeline.

Eduardo had scolded him for not telling her about marrying Kathy. Truth was, he hadn't expected to propose to her. He'd expected... he didn't know what he'd expected.

From the moment Curtis had called him about Madeline's surgery, the life that he'd thought made sense no longer did. He'd finally been content to move on and love another woman. He realized he'd love Madeline until the day he died, but somewhere in their bliss, they'd forgotten what really mattered.

They'd both walked away from their marriage. It wasn't as if she'd chosen Matt over him, though he'd accused her doing so. It was simply that she'd accepted their fate faster than he had.

They'd remained best friends over the years. His family still thought of her as family. Regan still took her shopping. Arianna would pay her a visit every time she was in town. His own mother made sure she had an invitation to dinner every Sunday night even if she didn't accept.

Now he was the one moving on and getting married, and she was divorced, alone, lonely, and... dying. He unwrapped his arms from Kathy and rolled out of bed.

He didn't want to fight with Madeline. Lord knew she didn't need anything to upset her. But he had to talk to her. He couldn't go through life knowing she was resentful to him for trying to take care of her.

He turned on the bathroom light and started the shower. He needed to feel the warm water pounding down on him.

Stripping out of his pajama bottoms, he looked in the mirror. There were dark circles under his eyes. His hair needed trimming, and he already needed to shave again.

He stepped into the shower and let the hot water burn away the pain wrenching inside of him.

What would have happened had they thought things through five years ago? Everyone had hard times. That's what life was about. He'd been a college student for almost ten years straight. During that time, his young wife had given birth to three children and worked two jobs to pay off his student loans.

Once he graduated, he had a hard time finding a school to hire him. Hadn't the plan been to get his master's degree and get the better job so he could support his growing family and Madeline could stay home? That was the plan. But it had all fallen apart.

The first of the big fights had happened on her birthday. Then the next a week later. He couldn't even remember who decided he should move out. All he knew was he was sleeping on a friend's couch. Then he'd moved in with his parents. After Arianna moved to New York and Regan moved back to Tennessee, they'd both moved into Arianna's house together. The two lost souls trying to piece their lives back. Regan pieced hers together faster than he had.

He turned off the water and stepped out of the shower. When the cold air hit him, he reached for the robe that hung on the back of the door and wrapped it around himself.

He'd wait until her parents left. Then he'd go to her and offer his support. No matter what came next, they shared a family. They were a family, even if they weren't married.

CHAPTER 12

*E*duardo stood in the hallway and listened to the sounds of his mother getting sick in the bathroom.

"Mom, are you okay?" he asked as she threw up for the third time since he'd awakened.

"I'm fine, baby," she said as he heard her again.

"I'm worried about you. Let me call Dad."

"Just get ready for school. You can't be late."

He stood there for a few more minutes with his ear pressed against the door and a pain in his chest that he didn't like. His mother was never sick, and he didn't know what he could do to help her. So he did as she'd asked and went about getting his shower and making sure everyone else was ready for school.

He made breakfast for Christian and Clara, and his mother a piece of dry toast. When she turned the corner into the kitchen, he went to her and helped her to a chair.

"Eat this." He set the plate down in front of her.

She gave it a look of consideration and then pushed it away. "I don't think I can."

"You've lost ten pounds already. You don't have a lot to lose. Eat it."

Madeline nodded as he went back to packing lunch for Clara. "Thank you guys for being here with me. It really helps me." She reached her hand out and covered Christian's. He only nodded his head. "So when is your choir concert?"

"In two weeks. I have extra practices next week. I have a note." She smiled. "Okay. We'll make sure you get there."

Eduardo handed Clara her lunch. "Okay, Mom. I made you some soup and it's in the fridge. You just have to warm it up. Don't forget your medicine and get in lots of fluids today. I'm going to call you between classes, and you'd better answer."

"Yes, sir."

"We'll be home by four." He bent down to kiss her cheek. "You're burning up." He put his hand to her head. "Mom, how long have you been like this?"

"Just since this morning."

"But you've been throwing up for three days."

"It's normal."

"I'm calling Dad." He pulled his cell phone from his pocket and she grabbed it from his hands.

"You will do no such thing."

His mother made eye contact with each of them. "This is normal. I'm okay. I have an appointment to see the doctor tomorrow. We'll see what they say. Maybe they can give me something. But I don't want you calling your father. Do you hear me?" She looked directly at Eduardo, who hesitantly nodded. "Okay."

"Why don't I just stay with you?" he offered. It was killing him to see her look so weak.

"I'd rather you get an education. And you'd better get to the bus."

～

CARLOS MISSED THE KIDS. THE MORNINGS WERE FUSS FREE, BUT quiet wasn't something he particularly enjoyed. For five years, he'd had the children at his house every other week. It had only been a few days, but he knew they'd be gone for weeks. However, with parent-teacher conferences coming up, it was giving him time to get his reports for each student in order.

Kathy laid her phone on the counter and pulled her travel mug from the cupboard. "I'm going to be late getting home. I have a meeting and then I'm going to run over to Regan's house. Audrey is going to meet us and discuss catering options."

"Sounds like a lovely time."

"Smart-ass." She bent to kiss him. "Be nice or I'll make you go."

"I have to get everything ready for conferences next week."

"Then this will work out great," she said just as his phone rang.

"Hey, Ed. Good morning." Carlos stacked the papers he'd scattered on the table and put them into his commuter bag. "How's everyone this morning?" He watched Kathy fill her coffee mug. "Good. I think it's good for you to be there. Do you need a ride home from school today?" He stood and walked to the sink to dump out his own mug. "Okay, I'll call you all tonight. I love you," he said and slid the phone into his shirt pocket.

"Everything okay?" Kathy asked as she buttered a bagel.

"Yep. He says everyone is doing great. Madeline is feeling good and they're glad they're staying with her." He wrapped his arms around her waist and laid a kiss on her neck. "You know, if you don't spend all night at my sister's house, we could get to bed early tonight."

She squirmed beneath his lips and laughed. "Mr. Keller..."

"Yes?"

She turned into his arms and pressed a soft, warm, and inviting kiss to his lips. "I promise I won't stay too long."

"I'm going to hold you to that."

Kathy glanced at her watch. "Oh, I'm going to be late." She kissed him again. "I love you."

"I love you too," he said as she pushed past him, grabbed her bag, and headed out the back door.

Carlos turned off the coffeepot.

His phone rang again and he pulled it from his pocket. The ID was from Christian's school.

"Hello," he said quickly. He'd never gotten a call from Christian's school. He hoped he wasn't sick or hurt.

"Dad?"

"Chris, what's wrong?" He pulled his bag over his shoulder and headed toward the back door.

"Did you talk to Ed this morning?"

"Yeah. He called when he got to school."

"Okay. So you know?" Carlos heard his son's voice calm.

Carlos clenched his teeth and felt the heat rise under his collar. "Well, why don't you tell me what I should know."

"That Mom is really sick."

Carlos was reaching for the car door, but he stopped. "Your mom is sick?"

"Yeah, I thought you said he told you."

"How sick, Chris?" He threw his bag into the passenger seat with a huff as he climbed into his car and began backing out of the driveway.

"She's been throwing up for the past four days. She's lost like ten pounds, Dad."

He shook his head. Damnit! What good was it to have Eduardo lying to him when he was supposed to be there to help?

Carlos looked down the road, checking for traffic. He turned sharply onto the street, narrowly evading the mailbox and the six-foot ditch on the side of the road. He swerved back and sucked in a breath. He needed to get a grip or he'd get himself killed, and then where would his children be?

"She's taking her medicine, right?"

"Yeah, that's what's making her sick." He sounded so young and frightened. "Dad, she's really, really sick."

He came to an abrupt stop at the stop sign at the end of the street. "Okay. You get to class. I'll check on her." Turning left would have taken him to work, but instead he turned right and headed toward Madeline.

CHAPTER 13

$\mathcal{C}$arlos had the foresight to call Curtis and ask what he should do.

"Antinausea medicine will help and so will ginger. You can get both of them at the drugstore or grocery store."

Carlos headed toward the drugstore just around the corner from Madeline's house.

"And what do I do to make her eat?"

"If she can start keeping things down, she'll eat. But you'd better keep an eye on her too. Anorexia is very common when patients can't keep food down."

"So they fixed her just so everything else would kill her?" He gripped the steering wheel as if bending it into a different shape would cure Madeline. "It seems like cutting off half of her should have been enough."

"Carlos, it isn't going to help her if you're upset."

"I know, I know. But damnit, she should have told me she was sick. I bought Ed a damn phone just for this reason, and he lies to me."

"She doesn't want to upset you."

"Well, it doesn't seem to be working, does it?" He pulled into the parking lot of the drugstore. "She can't die," he said on a sigh.

"Carlos, she's already past the hardest part. What did they say about the results?"

"They got all of the tumor. They said it looks good for her and she'll finish her round of chemo."

"The chemo is keeping everything at bay and killing off anything that might have lingered. Soon she'll be able to have the reconstruction done and she'll feel and look more normal. That will help her recovery. When she looks normal, her attitude will brighten. But for now she needs you and the kids to just be pillars of strength."

"You're right. Thanks."

"You're welcome. Hey, why don't you see if she'll come to Mom and Dad's on Sunday for dinner. Maybe Mom can get her to eat."

"Yeah, maybe I will."

"I love you, Bro. Take care of yourself too."

"I will," he promised before hanging up and walking into the store.

The woman behind the counter directed him to the medicines and herbs. He wasn't sure what the hell he was doing, but he gathered every bottle he thought would help her. Then he took it to the pharmacy, explained what he wanted, and the pharmacist handed him back only two bottles.

"This should be all she needs, and it won't interfere with her treatment."

After thanking the pharmacist, he found a book for Madeline to read. If he remembered correctly, Nora Roberts was her favorite, so he picked up the two books that were on the shelf. She'd like three or four of the gossip magazines, so he grabbed them. A Hershey's bar, it was her favorite too. After finding her a puzzle book, and her favorite lip balm, he headed toward the checkout.

Eighty-seven dollars later, he was back on the road toward Madeline's house.

CARLOS GATHERED THE BAGS OF ITEMS HE'D PURCHASED AND walked to the front door. He looked around the yard. No one had cleaned up the leaves from the fall, and he wondered if that bastard ex-husband of hers had even bothered to turn off the sprinklers before he abandoned her.

A branch was breaking on the tree near the bedroom window. That would need to be cut down before it broke the glass. He'd make a list, and he and the boys would take care of it.

Carlos rang the doorbell, stood, and waited. There had never been a day since he'd moved out of the house that it didn't feel odd to stand there and wait for someone to answer.

She didn't come to the door.

Carlos rang the bell again, and then pounded on the screen door. Still there was no answer. He walked to the garage and peered in the window. Her car was there. She must be inside.

He set the bags on the porch, and again rang the bell. When she didn't come, he took out his keys. It was a long shot, but he'd never taken the house key off his ring. Surely Matt had changed the locks. He slid the key into the lock and turned.

The door opened.

"Maddie! Maddie! Where are you?"

He stood for a moment and then he could hear her. She was in the bathroom and she was getting sick, again.

CARLOS DROPPED THE BAGS AT THE DOOR AND WENT TO HER.

He kept calling her name so he wouldn't frighten her. When he found her, she was sprawled on the floor of the bathroom in her robe. Her arms and head rested on the side of the bathtub.

"Maddie."

"Carlos, go home." She crawled toward the toilet. The movements were there, the noise was there, but she had nothing to throw up.

Carlos gathered her in his arms and carried her to her bedroom. She was so weak she didn't argue with him.

"What are you doing here? You should be at work." Her voice was weak and that didn't settle with him.

He needed to call work.

"I got you some stuff. I'll be right back." He grabbed the small trash can she kept by the bedside and set it next to her.

He called the school and convinced them he was sick, but the principal wasn't happy and made it perfectly clear.

He carried the bags to her room and found her sleeping. That had to be a positive, he thought. At least she was getting some rest and had stopped heaving.

The best thing for him to do was to make himself at home and do what he could for her while she slept. He brewed a pot of coffee, did the breakfast dishes, and mopped up the bathroom. If she was going to be spending time on the floor, it'd better be clean.

He'd finished his conference notes by the time he heard her stirring in her room, and he went to her.

Carlos carried in a tray with the soup he'd found in the fridge, some tea, and a few ginger pills. He set it on her nightstand and turned on the small lamp. "Are you feeling any better?"

"My stomach is sore."

"I'll bet." He closed the blind so that the light was soft. "Is that okay?"

"Yes. Thanks."

"Let's get you situated." He gathered her into his arms, and she clung to him. For a moment he held on to the feeling of her near him. He knew it was for strength, but a part of him felt a deeper connection.

He arranged pillows until she could sit up against them.

He handed her the pills and a glass of water. "Here, it's ginger. Curtis says to take them and they'll help with the nausea."

She nodded and took the pills.

CARLOS KICKED OFF HIS SHOES, PICKED UP THE BOWL HE'D CARRIED in, and walked around the other side of the bed.

Careful not to spill the contents of the bowl, he scooted across the mattress until he sat next to her. "Let's get something in your belly."

"Carlos, I can't eat," she said weakly.

"You need to try. You're not going to fight off anything if you don't keep up your strength."

He lifted the spoon to her lips, and she slurped then laid her head back on the pillow.

"Try some more." He lifted the spoon to her lips again and she took another sip. "Okay, now we're making progress."

This time when she laid her head back, it rested on his shoulder. Instinctively he kissed her forehead.

"So he told you I was sick? I asked him not to."

"Ed? No, he kept your secret."

Madeline turned her eyes up at him. "How did you know?"

"Christian called me from the school office because he was so worried about you." Gently he tilted her face with his fingers and looked down into her dark eyes. "You're not doing yourself any favors by having Ed lie to me about your condition."

"I didn't tell him to lie. I just told him to tell you I was okay. Which I am, by the way."

"No, you're not. When is your next doctor appointment?"

"Tomorrow."

"I'm taking you."

Madeline tried to sit up and turn away from him, but Carlos guided her back to his shoulder. Then he lifted the spoon of soup back to her lips and she took another sip.

"You need to be at work. You worked too damn hard to get that job. You'd better keep it," she argued.

"For your sake I will. If it weren't for you, I wouldn't have the education to even have the job. But for once in your life, admit you need some help."

She sat silently for a moment. "This was never supposed to happen." He heard the quiver in her voice and then felt her body shake as the tears rolled down her cheeks. "I've never been sick a day in my life."

"I know, honey." He set the bowl of soup on the other nightstand and gathered her in his arms and held her against his chest.

"Look at me. I'm a mess. My skin is pasty, my boobs are missing, and now my hair is falling out in clumps." She threw a hand in the air. "My husband left me and is marrying someone else..."

"Wait." He adjusted to see her better. "Matt is getting married?"

She nodded. "And she's pregnant."

"Son of a bitch," he said through gritted teeth. His hand formed into a fist at his side. If it were any other time, he'd have found a wall to put a hole in. "He was having an affair?"

She nodded again. "It doesn't matter." She adjusted to rest against him again.

"It does matter. You don't do that. You don't marry someone and then change your mind." He couldn't control his anger, and now he wasn't sure if it was directed at Matt for leaving Madeline or Madeline for leaving him five years ago. Sitting there with her in his arms was confusing his thought process.

"I know I should be upset, but I'm not. I never loved him. Not like I should have." Her shoulders dropped and her face turned into his chest. He could feel her breath on his neck and his heartbeat grew faster. "Not like I loved you."

A sharp pain resonated in his chest. "You should get some

more rest." In his present state of mind he'd better not say any more. He kissed her forehead. "I'll be here when you wake up," he promised her as she rolled to her side.

He took the quilt from the foot of the bed and laid it over her. His mother had made it for them when Christian was born. It meant the world that she still used it and kept it close.

CHAPTER 14

While Madeline slept he made plans for the next day. He'd call in a substitute for one more day. He could afford to do that. They'd go to the doctor, and he'd hear for himself how she was doing. From where he stood, it didn't look like she was doing very well at all.

He met the kids at the bus stop when they got out of school and drove them back to Madeline's. When Christian and Clara had made it into the house, he took hold of Eduardo's arm and turned him toward him.

"You've been lying to me." He narrowed his stare at his son and he could see anger rise in Eduardo's eyes. "She's lost ten pounds and has been sick for days. Her hair is falling out in clumps. She can hardly walk she's so weak, and she sleeps all day. What part of that is fine to you?"

Eduardo pulled his arm back from Carlos' grasp. "Dad, she didn't want me to say anything to you."

"You needed to."

"I was doing what she asked me to do. You're so busy with Kathy, she didn't want to worry you."

"Too late." It all boiled in his stomach. Madeline, Kathy, the kid—it all seemed so complicated.

"Why are you here? Did she call you?"

Carlos shook his head. "No, your brother called me from school because he was so worried about her. Ed, you needed to tell me. You're not here during the day to take care of her. She needs more than you just making her breakfast and making sure she's getting into bed each night."

"Dad! Is that all you think I do?" His voice had risen to match Carlos anger.

Carlos rested his hand gently on his son's shoulder. "No. No, I know you're taking good care of her. I'm sorry." He raked his fingers through his hair and let out a breath. "It kills me to see her like this."

"Trust me. I know. I'm scared that every morning I'm going to go in to wake her up and she won't. It's almost a relief to hear her throwing up because I know at least she's alive. I watch her when she falls asleep on the couch trying to help us with our homework. I watch her chest rise and fall. I ask her every morning to let me stay here, but it's Mom, she refuses."

"Of course she does."

"I'm sure this is what happens on those meds. I asked Uncle Curtis and he said she sounds normal. But it's hard to watch."

"It is." He put his arm around his son's shoulders and walked with him toward the house. The emotion of it all mixed with the pride that he had in his son. "I'm taking off tomorrow to go to the doctor's appointment with her. I'll find out all I can. If you have questions, let me know and I'll try to answer them or get answers to them." He kissed his son's head as they walked through the front door of the home they all once shared.

Carlos held open the screen as Eduardo walked through, and he let out a breath. If only he didn't have to turn back around and leave to go back to his own house.

· · ·

IT WAS ALMOST NINE O'CLOCK WHEN HE RETURNED HOME. KATHY sat at the kitchen table with an empty plate in front of her. A full plate sat in front of the other chair.

Her arms were crossed in front of her and her foot tapped on the wood floor. They hadn't had a fight yet in their relationship, but he had a feeling they were about to.

The color in Kathy's cheeks deepened and she inhaled a deep breath. "I came home as quickly as I could. I left Audrey's house and made a mad dash home to make you a special dinner and spend the evening with you." She stood and dumped her plate into the sink. Bracing her hands on the counter, she looked out the window, over the sink, and out into the darkness. "Do I even have to ask where you were?"

"Kath, I'm sorry."

"I'm done with sorry, Carlos." She spun around. "You asked me to marry you. Do you even remember that?"

"Kathy…"

"Why in the hell did you ask me? Why did you lead me to believe that there was a future with us?" She walked to the table and picked up the full plate of food. She then dumped it into the sink, turned on the disposal, and began to sob.

Carlos moved to her and laid his hand on her back. He reached around her and turned off the disposal and absorbed the sound of her sobbing.

Kathy shook her head. "I knew from the moment I met you that I wasn't Madeline. I don't look like her. I'm not as smart as her. I'm not anything like her."

"No you're not," he said softly turning her toward him. "You're completely you, and that's what I love."

"But since she's been sick, you've done nothing but spend your time with her."

"I know."

"It's as if I don't exist."

"That's not true." He pulled her into his arms, and she rested her head against his chest.

"I miss you. I miss the kids. I feel like her husband left her so my family left me."

His heart was racing. He hadn't meant to hurt her, but he was. Sooner or later Kathy was going to break, he'd known that, and he suspected she'd hit her breaking point. But he couldn't leave Maddie. She needed him too. The only thing he could do was be honest with Kathy.

"Listen," he said pushing her back to look into her damp blue eyes. "I love you. So I need to tell you what's going on. I need to be there for Madeline. I need to get her through this, for the kids." She nodded. "She's one of my oldest friends, and I share with her the one thing that has always made me whole. My family. I never meant to hurt you by caring for her."

"I hate that I'm jealous." She wiped at her eyes and pressed her body closer to his. "I hate that it bothers me."

He pulled her to him again. "You have the kindest heart."

"It's getting a workout lately. I can't shake it and it bothers me."

"I know." He ran his hand over her hair as if the touch could take away her pain, but he had so much of his own, no amount of soft strokes with his hand was going to heal her heart. "I'm taking her to the doctor tomorrow. She's very weak, and I'm worried about her. Curtis says it all sounds normal, but she's never down like this."

Kathy pulled back and looked up at him. A crease formed between her brows as it always did when something worried her. "Are the kids too much on her? They could come back home."

"No. Actually, I think they keep her going. But I want to hear for myself what's going on and what's next. I owe that to her and the kids."

Kathy ran her fingers under her eyes, smearing the black

mascara smudges that had formed. "I know my throwing temper tantrums doesn't seem like I care, but I do."

"I know you do. And I'm being totally up front with you, even if it seems like I'm not."

"I know you are. I just can't believe Matt wouldn't stick around."

Carlos let out a breath and backed away from Kathy. He picked up the glass of wine she'd left on the table, which she'd obviously poured for him, and drank it down. The sweetness landed in his gut, but the alcohol did nothing to dull the pain he was feeling. "He's getting married."

"Married?"

"Yep." He picked up the bottle and filled the glass again, hoping a second helping would ease the anger he had brewing over the man he once called his best friend. "They're having a baby, isn't that sweet?" The words burned against his tongue.

"Oh." She covered her mouth. "That's awful."

"Some stand-up guy." He finished the second glass of wine and set down the glass.

"I really think I should go spend some time with her. I need to let her know I support her."

Carlos gathered her back in his arms. "That's what amazes me about you. You're so compassionate."

"I don't feel amazing or compassionate. I feel petty."

He laughed and kissed her forehead. "You're nothing of the sort."

"I'll wait until you know what's going on with her."

He nodded. "Curtis thinks we should bring her to dinner at Mom and Dad's on Sunday."

The tightening in her jaw didn't go unnoticed, but she smiled and batted away tears. "I think that would be wonderful for her."

"I'll talk to her about it tomorrow. But for now..." He hoisted her up to his waist, and she wrapped her legs around him. He planted a kiss on her lips that made her go pliant in his arms.

"Didn't you say something about going to bed early?" he asked with a playful rise of his eyebrows.

"That was the idea."

He held her tight, pressing his face into her shoulder and wishing he could clear his mind of Madeline. "Let's go mess up those sheets."

CHAPTER 15

*M*adeline had paced the floor in the kitchen from the moment she'd awoken until the kids had left for the school bus. How was she going to talk Carlos out of going to her appointment with her? No possible excuse she could come up with was going to hold.

The point was, he was going to go whether she wanted him to or not. He was going to drive her in her own damn car if she refused to get in his. And no matter what, she knew it was the right thing to do. After all, she'd gone through the surgery without having told anyone only to find him by her bedside.

Carlos had given up everything in his life to take care of her— she owed him that much, to let him go and ask his own questions. Besides, it would be good to have more than one set of ears listening to what they had to tell her.

Madeline finished as much of her breakfast as she could. Her nerves twisted her stomach. With a gulp of her cold coffee, she took her medicine and then lay back down on her bed. Already she was exhausted. He'd be here there in two hours. There was plenty of time to take a nap before she showered and got ready.

"Maddie!" She heard her name called in her quiet house. It was familiar—a comforting sound. "Maddie!"

She sat up quickly, her heart racing at a record pace. She sucked in a breath when she realized she'd been alone when she'd fallen asleep.

"There you are," Carlos said as he leaned against the doorjamb to her bedroom.

Madeline rested her hand on her chest and calmed herself down. She looked him over, standing in the doorway as he had a million times before. He looked just as relaxed now, as a guest, as he always had as her husband. That made the uneasy feeling in her stomach return.

Carlos shifted his weight. "I knocked, rang the bell, knocked again." He laughed. "It's a damn good thing that husband of yours never thought I was enough of a threat to change the locks."

She rubbed her eyes. "What time is it?"

"Time to go." He walked closer to the side of the bed.

"I didn't mean to sleep this long." She kicked back the covers and landed her feet on the floor. "I need to take a shower."

"You look fine. We don't have time for a shower."

We don't have time for a shower. He didn't mean it the way she heard it, but it warmed her just the same. Oh, how she wished they didn't have to go to the appointment and they could stay right there. Her mind had been filled with him holding her in his arms, just as he had done the day before when he fed her soup.

Why was this man with dark chocolate eyes and handfuls of wavy black hair not her husband anymore? Where had it all gone so terribly wrong? She couldn't even remember.

Madeline swallowed hard and fought back the sadness that hovered in her chest. He belonged to Kathy now, just as she'd belonged to Matt for so many years.

"Are you all right?" He stepped even closer to her.

"I'm fine." She smiled up at him then leaned back, away from him. She needed her space. It was as if the cancer wasn't the only thing trying to kill her. Her emotions were doing their best to finish the job. "Let me get changed and I'll be right out."

"Okay." He lingered with those dark eyes on her just a moment longer before he left the bedroom and shut the door behind him.

MADELINE TAPPED HER FINGERS ON THE SEAT BELT BUCKLE AS Carlos pulled the car into the parking lot of the medical building. Nerves had gripped every muscle in her body and squeezed them until she felt numb. She fidgeted, trying to keep herself calm. It wasn't the doctor's visit making her nervous. It was the feeling that kept creeping into her heart when Carlos was around.

He must have sensed her anxiety. He placed his hand over hers until she stopped tapping her fingers, then put his hand back on the steering wheel. "So do you have any plans this weekend?"

"No. I don't make too many plans anymore."

He turned his head to look at her. "Come to dinner at Mom and Dad's."

"No."

He adjusted behind the wheel and drove down the aisle, looking for a parking space. "Now you've hurt my feelings."

"I didn't mean to. I just don't think I belong there, that's all."

"What makes you say that?"

"You have a fiancée, Carlos. You don't need me at a family dinner."

"But you are family."

"I'm ex-family."

"We've never made you feel that way," he said sharply as he pulled into a space.

"No. You and your family have been very gracious to me. They always have been. But I can't do that to Kathy. She's sharing you enough, and I don't want to jeopardize her kindness toward me either."

Carlos pulled into a parking space and put the car in park. "Kathy knows I'm inviting you, and she thinks it will be nice for you to be with everyone."

"Really?" She turned her head to capture his stare. "She said that?"

"Yes, she said that."

Madeline shook her head. It shouldn't have bothered her that the woman was so willing to accept her, but it did. There was a part of her that wanted to be ex-family. She didn't want to think they still liked her and accepted her. It would have been easier if they didn't. But that wasn't how the Keller family worked. She let out a deep breath. "You are marrying one amazing woman."

"I sure am. C'mon."

Those few words stuck her like a knife. What had she expected? He loved Kathy, she knew that. But she realized he'd been so attentive to her, she'd let her thoughts wander toward the absurd as if he'd ever give it all up for her, again.

Carlos climbed out of the car and walked around to her side. He opened her door and extended his hand. She pushed it away and climbed out of the car. Without even waiting for him, she started toward the building.

"Maddie," Carlos called after her. "Wait." He reached for her arm and turned her toward him. "What just happened? What's gotten into you?"

"Nothing." How could she possibly tell him her heart was hurting because she still loved him and always had? How could she tell him that, when she knew he was marrying a woman who was so much more than she was? Kathy wasn't petty, but Madeline was finding out that she was. Obviously Kathy wasn't the jealous type either, but the green-eyed monster was eating Madeline one gracious comment at a time.

Carlos let go of her arm, but he kept his eyes focused on her. "Don't lie to me. I know you so much better than you think."

He did. He knew her inside and out and vice versa. So why couldn't she let it go? Why couldn't she just let him be happy?

"I'm sorry. I'm not handling all of this too well."

"Why should you?" He pulled her to him. "Cancer isn't just something that comes and goes. You have to fight it. You're doing that. That doctor is going to tell us you're doing great. I know this."

She nodded against his chest, taking in the comfort he offered.

"Besides." He brushed his hand down her back, causing a guilty little shiver there. "You've never backed down from anything. You're not going to back down now."

No, she'd never backed down from anything until the day one of them decided he needed to move out. Now, she couldn't even remember who'd mentioned it first.

CHAPTER 16

*M*adeline changed into her gown and lay on the exam table. Then she called for Carlos, who had waited just beyond the door.

When he walked into the room, he smiled at her, but she knew it was only to keep her calm. There was a fire burning beyond his eyes. Worry was consuming him as much as jealousy was consuming her.

He took her hand in his. "The doctor is in the next room. He'll be in, in a few minutes."

Madeline nodded. She wished she could explain her feelings to him, but what would it matter? He was being friendly. He'd always been friendly when it came to her. "Are you sure Kathy is okay with me coming to dinner?"

"Of course."

She nodded. "I think that would be great. I'll be there."

The worry in his eyes changed, and at that moment she knew he was happy. His beautiful smile had her heart racing, again. She remembered the first time he'd ever smiled at her. Tall, dark, and handsome was an understatement. She'd fallen in love with his smile, and then his eyes, and then that deep voice that cracked because it hadn't settled into the fifteen-year-old body of the man she'd later fall in love with.

He stroked her knuckles with his thumb. "I'll come by and get you."

"No. I'll meet you there."

"Are you sure?"

"Yes. It'll be best for everyone."

"Are you already planning an escape?"

"Me?" She laughed. "No. I was offering you one."

The door opened, and the doctor walked through with a clipboard in his arm. "Madeline, how are you?"

"I'm doing fine." She shook his hand.

"Dr. Martin," he introduced himself, turning to Carlos and holding out his hand.

"Carlos Keller," he said shaking the doctor's hand.

"Carlos is my ex-husband, and"—she turned her eyes toward him—"he's my best friend. He's helping me get through this."

Carlos gave her hand a squeeze. She wondered if it felt as weird to him to call her his ex-wife. No matter how long it had been, it still squeezed at her heart to say it.

"It must be working." Dr. Martin looked at the papers on the clipboard. "Your white blood count looks better than it did right after the surgery. Your weight is down though."

"She sleeps a lot and she's not eating," Carlos said quickly as if he were making sure she didn't leave anything out.

Dr. Martin made a note in the chart. "Madeline, do you think this is worse than before?"

She bit down on her lip, looked up at Carlos, and then back at the doctor. "Well, I do lose energy pretty fast, and I throw up at least once a day."

"We'll get you something to help you with your nausea and something to get that white blood count up."

She nodded.

"Now let's look at you." Dr. Martin moved toward her and Carlos stepped back.

Carlos looked at her. "I'll wait outside."

"Please stay," she heard herself say, though she hadn't planned on asking him to.

"Are you sure?"

She understood the fear in his eyes. When he saw what they'd done to her in surgery, he might want to stop coming around. But she nodded.

The doctor pushed back her gown, and Madeline heard Carlos gasp. She clenched her fists at her sides. What had he expected? Did he really think she'd have let him stand there and ogle her bare chest had it been intact?

Madeline felt the tears well in her eyes, and she turned her head to make sure he couldn't see them. He'd never look at her the way he once had. How could he?

"This looks good," Dr. Martin said as he covered her back up. "Have you given consideration to reconstruction?"

She felt Carlos shift at her side, and when she looked up at him, she saw the telltale sign of the line that creased between his brows. He was uncomfortable.

Good. So was she.

"Oh, I want reconstruction. I just want to finish this first." She forced her voice to be steady so Carlos could hear that she'd be fine. She didn't need him taking care of her forever. He didn't have to feel sorry for her. One day, very soon, she'd be a complete woman again.

Dr. Martin nodded. "That's perfectly understandable." He made more notes and then filled out a prescription and handed it to her. "I think you're doing great. We'll do more blood work in a few weeks and more x-rays. If this doesn't help with the nausea and the energy levels, I want you to call me. I want you to be very careful during this time of year and stay healthy. With your white blood count still a little off, a simple cold could become something more complicated," he warned.

"Should I keep the kids from her?" Carlos asked, his voice filled with panic.

"No. But make sure they keep themselves clean. Have them take extra showers and wash their hands often. They are most likely to bring home germs. We just want to take as many precautions as possible."

"What about her hair?" He asked another question she had forgotten to ask. There were some benefits to having him there, she decided. Carlos kept his eyes on the doctor. "She says it's starting to fall out."

Dr. Martin nodded and made more notes. "It's perfectly normal for some people to lose their hair during chemotherapy." He turned toward Madeline. "This will be your call, of course. If it has started, likely it will keep coming out. It's going to hurt." He considered his words. "Not painfully, but imagine you have a sunburn on your scalp, and it itches and hurts. You understand, right?"

"Yes." Madeline swallowed hard. She hadn't thought about the process of it falling out, just that it would, and quickly. "So I'll be bald?"

"Hair comes out in patches. You'll more than likely want to take the clippers to it. Don't shave it with a razor." He lifted his eyes to Carlos. "It'll cause infection."

Carlos nodded his understanding, but she saw the corners of his lips turn down. The very thought of how ugly she was going to be—breastless and hairless—obviously made him sick.

Dr. Martin looked back at Madeline. "You can cover your head with a scarf, hat, or wig to keep your head warm if you want. Especially during the winter, you'll want to do that to keep your body heat in. As for looks, many women cover their heads. It's up to you."

He gave his notes another look then lifted his eyes to her.

Pushing his shoulders back, he smiled. That gave her some confidence. The man looked pleased with her checkup. "Madeline, call me if you need anything or if you have questions."

Madeline forced a grin. "Thank you." She wanted to feel as positive as the doctor looked.

"Mr. Keller, it was nice to meet you. I'm glad to see Madeline has a good support team."

"She does, sir," Carlos said as he looked at her. "Our children and I are here for her." For the first time she saw something in his eyes she hadn't seen in more than five years. There was a peace that shaded them. The kind that had been there before when times were hard, but he still had loved her. A lump caught in her throat.

Dr. Martin nodded and left the room. Carlos helped her from the table.

"I'll wait for you outside," he offered and headed for the door.

"Carlos." He turned back to her. "Thank you for coming with me. I was trying to think of every excuse to make you not come, but I'm glad I couldn't come up with any."

"I wouldn't have listened to them anyway."

She nodded and smiled. "I know. I just want you to know this means the world to me."

He tucked his bottom lip in and nodded. He was nervous; she knew his tells. Madeline knew he wanted to hug her, to kiss away all her pain, but he stood across the room and finally opened the door.

"I'll be out in a few minutes."

He left the room, and Madeline sat for a moment. She pulled off the drape and looked down at her disfigured body. The curves were gone and there was nothing left, much like her life in general. The man she'd always loved had found someone new, and she winced when she realized she'd been the one to encourage it. The man who had held her hand the past five years had started his life over. And here she was, hoping that every day she'd wake up and get to spend more time with her children.

Madeline reached for her shirt and slipped her arms through the sleeves. The fabric fought her and she pushed her arm through. But it wasn't the shirt, it was the unsettling feeling that was making her tense. The thoughts that crowded her mind, wishing Kathy had never happened into his life and that Matt had walked out of hers much sooner. The very thought hurt as much as the scars on her body as they healed.

She could hear Carlos' voice carry down the hall as he spoke with someone passing by her door. He was everything she'd ever wanted, and he always did what she'd asked him to do. Carlos loved her. He'd married her. The agreement was that she'd support them so he could go to school and get a good job. Carlos did just that. And she must have told him to walk away, because he wasn't the kind of man to walk away without being pushed. And now he was marrying someone else because she'd asked him to move on.

Madeline pressed her hand to her flat chest. As it was, even if she won the battle against the disease that wanted to kill her, she'd still never win back the love of her life.

CHAPTER 17

$\mathcal{M}$adeline ambled up the front steps of Alan and Emily Keller's house. She couldn't remember a time she'd been more nervous. Even the day she'd gone to the doctor's office to confirm that she had cancer, she wasn't as jittery.

She blew out a breath. There was no reason for her to be uncomfortable. Not a day had passed since she was fifteen years old that the Kellers hadn't been completely accepting of her.

Madeline had turned down dinner invitations every month for five years. She'd been surrounded by Emily, Regan, and Arianna at every social event for her children for those same five years. She was at the fiftieth wedding anniversary party for Alan and Emily. When Zach's father died, she and the kids were at the funeral and reception to help. She helped Arianna host Regan's baby shower. Matt had even taken her to New York to see Arianna perform more than once. This was as much her family as her children were.

So why was she so tied up in knots?

In her closet she'd found the hat she'd bought for Regan's wedding. She hadn't worn it then, but it looked casual enough she figured she'd get away with wearing it to Sunday dinner. Only that morning she'd taken a mirror and looked at the back of her head. Her hair looked horrible. It was time to consider doing something about it. She tugged the hat down more snugly.

When the door opened, Clara greeted her.

"Mommy!" She clung to her and Madeline laughed.

"I dropped you off at your dad's house yesterday. It's only been eighteen hours since you've seen me."

"I know." Clara smiled up at her. "I just missed you."

All of the knots in her muscles relaxed; she was at home with her children here. "I missed you too."

Clara walked her through the front door by the hand and back to the family room where everyone had gathered around the television.

"Super Bowl," Clara whispered.

"I had completely forgotten," Madeline whispered back.

A roar erupted from everyone in the room when the team they'd been rooting for missed the field goal.

"Damn! When am I going to pick a team that has a chance?" Alan sat back in his recliner and looked up, noticing her first. His eyes lit up, and he struggled from his chair to be the first to greet her. "Well, look who graces our presence again."

"Alan, how are you?"

"I'm old." He kissed her cheek and then looked her directly in the eye. "How are you?"

"I'm going to be just fine."

"I know you are." He patted her cheek and stepped back as her sons gathered around her. Each member of the family kissed her and gave her a hug. Regan held her tightly, and Madeline could feel her body shake from tears.

"Don't be sad for me," Madeline spoke softly in her ear.

"I can't help it. I didn't know you were sick, and I really think I should have been there for you."

"You have a new person to think about. Tyler needs you more

than I do." She kissed Regan on the cheek. "Thank you for worrying though."

Regan stepped back and wiped her eyes. "I'm overly emotional lately."

"It's lack of sleep. I remember it well."

"All he does is eat. I never sleep anymore."

"It won't be forever and you'll miss it." She looked around the room at her nearly grown children. Regan would soon look back on it and wonder where the time had gone.

"That's what everyone keeps telling me."

"Hello, Madeline." The soft female voice came from the direction of the kitchen, and Madeline looked up to see Kathy standing only a few feet away with a tight smile directed toward her.

"Hello, Kathy," she said returning the smile, realizing they were both incredibly uncomfortable in each other's presence.

Madeline had met her a few times. Kathy had been there for Regan's baby shower, the first Keller family event Kathy had attended. It had only been four months earlier, but to Madeline it seemed like a lifetime ago. Back then, she was pleased to meet Kathy. Her heart had been full of optimism for Carlos. She'd been happy for him.

Now as she stood before the small blonde with her thick, full hair and her full chest. She envied her—not so much for the beauty she possessed and Madeline had lost, but because Carlos loved her.

Kathy took a hesitant step toward her. "I'm glad Carlos convinced you to come."

"I wasn't sure I should."

"You're part of the family," Kathy reminded her.

"Thank you."

It was then she realized she hadn't seen Carlos. She glanced toward the living room, but he wasn't there. Her face must have shown her thoughts.

"He ran to the store to get some more milk."

Madeline nodded. Regan moved by her with Tyler in her arms.

"I thought you could use this." She lifted her son toward Madeline, who took the baby and cradled him close to her empty chest. The warmth from his body filled her. The scent of baby lotion filled her nose and calmed her nerves.

"You have no idea."

CARLOS PUSHED THROUGH THE BACK DOOR, BAGS OF GROCERIES slipping from his fingers.

Kathy raced toward him and grabbed a bag before it could fall. "What did you get?"

"I couldn't help it. They had ice cream on sale." He grinned.

"You are no help to my waistline." She kissed him on the lips and helped Emily unload the bags. "She's in the other room," Kathy said quietly as she tilted her head toward Carlos.

"Really?" A surge of mixed emotions ran though him. He was happy. He'd wanted her to be there more than he could have admitted, but even though Kathy was smiling, the sadness in her eyes burned him. How could he have such contrasting emotions?

Kathy nodded. "Go see her."

He moved to her and placed his hands on her cheeks. "Are you okay with this?"

"Yes."

"I love you."

"I love you, too."

Carlos kissed her softly and then went in search of Madeline.

Chaos enveloped the room where everyone he loved sat watching the greatest football game of the year. But in the corner, the mother of his children rocked his tiny nephew, gazing down upon him. She was beautiful.

The thought hit him hard. He tried to shake it away, but it

lodged there. He remembered her holding Eduardo just as she held Tyler.

Madeline had been twenty-one and just had their first child. Most people at that age would have been panicking about everything, but not Madeline. She took it all in stride and had patience he'd never seen in any other woman. Not even his mother had patience like his wife's. Ex-wife, he had to remind himself.

"Park your butt or go somewhere else," Alan said to him, and he realized he was standing in plain sight of everyone, gazing at Madeline.

She looked up at him and smiled. He walked toward her and knelt down by the chair.

"He is so precious," she murmured as Carlos touched Tyler's soft cheek.

"He really is, isn't he?"

"I'm so glad I came. I needed this so much. Maybe on my bad days I'll just go over to Regan's house."

"She'd love that." He looked up at her and caught the love and patience that radiated from her eyes. She looked much better than she had earlier that week.

"Dinner is ready." Kathy's voice filled the room, but Carlos heard the tension in it, and when he looked up he saw the pain in her eyes again. But she smiled and stepped aside as his family filtered through the house toward the dining room.

"Good, my team is losing," Alan protested as Eduardo helped him up from his chair.

Zach reached out his hands to take Tyler from Madeline. "I'll take him."

"Would I be horribly out of line if I asked to hold him during dinner? You have no idea how much this is helping me."

"I think that would be fine," Zach said, smiling down at her as Regan placed her hand on her husband's shoulder.

Carlos helped her up and walked with her to the dining room.

He kept to her side, a hand on the low of her back to steady her. She wasn't weak, but it felt necessary to guide her with such a small and wonderful gift sleeping in her arms.

He pulled her chair out, and as she sat, he looked for the next open chair. A sharp pain pierced his chest when he realized his empty chair was across the table, next to his fiancée.

Kathy's eyes were lowered and the pain increased. He was hurting her, and yet he couldn't help it.

CHAPTER 18

*D*inner around the Keller table was as she always remembered it. It was noisy, full of discussions of work, school, and news of Arianna's latest adventures in New York.

Curtis had been the last to arrive, just as they'd all sat down at the table. Madeline sat between her sons and across from her daughter, who sat next to her father and he next to his fiancée. She knew she should feel out of place, but she didn't. She wished she'd taken them up on dinner offers sooner.

"Are you sure you don't want me to take him from you?" Regan asked as Madeline struggled to lift her fork to her mouth without dropping food on Tyler.

"Please, leave him. This has been the very best therapy."

"I'm glad."

"How is your recovery going?" Emily asked in her calm, motherly manner.

"I think it's going well. The doctor gave me some medicine to help my blood count and to keep me from getting sick." She cut another piece of ham and managed it into her mouth.

"I'm glad you're getting better."

"Thank you."

"Look." Eduardo smiled at her. "She's eating."

Madeline looked down at her plate and realized she'd eaten half the food on it while she cooed over the baby in her arms.

"I guess I am."

"Good, you're getting too skinny," Carlos added.

"Oh, I don't think there will ever be a day I think that."

"You never would. You're too hard on yourself."

"Maybe." She managed another fork of food to her mouth.

"You are such a natural," Zach added his opinion. "Did you always manage to be so calm around babies?"

"She was always good with babies and kids. I don't think she was sick a day when she was pregnant," Carlos offered.

"And that wives' tale about having heartburn if you child had a lot of hair didn't apply to me. Ed had more hair than most full-grown men." She gazed at her son, who shook his head as he drank down his milk.

"Oh, he was hairy like a monkey," Regan reminisced.

"C'mon, that's gross," Eduardo piped up and they all laughed.

Carlos laughed. "Oh, and you were enormous!"

"Dad!"

"You were. You were fat and round. I don't know how you're mother managed to carry you for an extra four days."

"He was nine pounds." She laughed as she said it. "Talk about being all baby."

"And you carried him all up front. To look at you from behind, you wouldn't even have noticed she was pregnant," Curtis added to the conversation.

Carlos threw his napkin at his brother. "What were you doing looking at her from the back?"

"I was nineteen. I looked at every woman from the back."

The family laughed. Everyone but Kathy, who looked at her plate as she ate.

. . .

AFTER DINNER WAS FINISHED AND THE MEN HAD RETURNED TO THE football game, Madeline walked into the kitchen, where Emily and Kathy sat at the table with cups of coffee. "Thank you for a wonderful evening."

Emily stood and kissed her on the cheeks. "I'm so glad you finally came."

"So am I." She turned toward Kathy, who had stood too. "Thank you so much for being so kind and letting me join you all. It means the world to me that you're so kindhearted and let me be such a big part of Carlos' life. I know I've been a real pain lately."

"Oh, no. You're very important to him. You're part of our family," Kathy said with a smile that reminded Madeline just how kind a person she really was, but also with a tightness to her lips that let Madeline know that as welcome as she'd felt in her presence, it wasn't more than a one-time deal.

"I'm going to talk to the kids about going back to our normal schedule. I know he misses them, and I have to start back to work in a week or so. It's helped me having them around, but they need to be with you both too."

"Well, if you wouldn't mind, could we have them next week? I've planned for pictures. Engagement pictures, actually, but I'm not marrying just him, so I want the kids in the pictures too."

The thought gnawed at her. Kathy was right. She wasn't marrying just Carlos. She was marrying the whole family. Madeline swallowed back the pain of the thought and smiled. "I think that sounds nice."

"I'm glad you're feeling better. I know how he worries about you."

"Well, I think things are looking up. Hopefully by next Christmas I'll be cancer free and I'll be able to go to the company Christmas party in a strappy number and show off my new cleavage." She laughed, but it was forced because no matter what her hair or body looked like, she wouldn't be on the arm of the man she loved, and that hurt even worse.

CHAPTER 19

Kathy had sunk into the passenger seat of Carlos' car like a deflated balloon when the kids went home with Madeline. The fewer people she had around her, the better off she would be.

She sat with her hands clenched in her lap, listening to Carlos go on and on about how good he thought Madeline looked and how wonderful it was to have her at dinner.

He tapped his fingers on the steering wheel to the beat of the song on the radio. "I think I'll have to make sure Regan goes by a few times and takes Tyler to see her. I think that was the best part. She looked so comfortable with him in her arms."

He was positively ecstatic about the evening, and the very sound of his happy voice was raking across her nerves. The moment they pulled into the driveway, Kathy grabbed her purse and headed into the house while Carlos grabbed the bags of leftover ice cream from the trunk and put them away in the freezer. By the time he'd made it to their bedroom she'd put on her pajamas and brushed through her hair.

"Turning in early?"

She pulled back the sheets. "It's nine o'clock. I have an early meeting in the morning."

"I have some papers to grade. I'll come to bed in just a little bit," he said, moving toward her and kissing her. She couldn't help but flinch when his lips touched her.

"Are you okay?"

"I'm fine." She meant for it to sound sincere, but it came out snappy. She looked away and swung her feet under the sheets. "Please turn off the light when you walk out."

When she heard the door to his office close, she began to sob. Jealousy was ugly when it reared its nasty head. Jealousy on her was worse. But she couldn't help it. Did he know how he looked at Madeline? Did he know how he spoke of her? Kathy had sat by him all evening, but did he even notice as he sat and looked at his ex-wife?

If he'd noticed all of that, he would have stopped. He wasn't the kind of man to ignore the woman he loved. But that hit her too. Perhaps she wasn't the woman he loved after all.

She pounded her fist into the pillow and then dropped her head onto it. They were getting married. Madeline was doing better. She had to fight the ugliness of jealousy and make it go away. She'd hate herself if she didn't, and she'd hate him too.

MADELINE WOKE TO A GLORIOUS SUNRISE. SHE SUCKED IN A BREATH and let it out slow. She hadn't felt so good in months. Dinner at the Kellers' was just what she had needed—and holding little Tyler, well, that had made her night.

The sounds of her children moving about the house made her even happier. She pulled on her robe, slipped her feet into her slippers, and headed to the kitchen.

Eduardo handed her a piece of toast and kissed her cheek. "Mom, I think you're glowing."

"What are you making?"

"I made some eggs. They just wanted cereal."

"Can you make me some too?"

He turned to her and studied her close. "Really?"

The other sets of eyes at the table looked up at her.

Madeline smiled at each of them. "Yes, really. Today I feel like eating."

"Then I will make you eggs." He moved back to the refrigerator and took out the carton as she sat down and enjoyed the morning with her family.

Once they'd left for school, Madeline used the energy she had and changed her bedding, vacuumed the living room, and ran a load of laundry. Within an hour, she'd used every ounce of adrenaline she had and decided it was time for a shower.

She wasn't sure she'd ever get used to seeing herself naked. They'd taken out the stitches, and now she was left with only scars where her breasts had been. The best idea was just to not look down, but it was hard to divert her eyes as she ran soap over her body.

She poured shampoo in her hand and worked it through her hair. But it felt different. She massaged the shampoo on her head, and when she pulled her hands back, the amount of hair still stuck to her fingers was more than ever before.

She quickly rinsed off, climbed out of the shower, and wrapped her robe around her, leaving the tangle of hair clogging the tub drain. She took a deep breath and faced the mirror. It was then that she saw what she'd wanted to pretend hadn't been happening. Her hair had thinned to the point that she could see right through it. It made her look even sicker. It made her feel sicker too.

At one in the afternoon, Carlos called to check on her. When she couldn't hide the tears in her voice, he said he'd be over as soon as he could.

"Carlos, don't you dare. I'm fine. I'm just being a little vain."

She rubbed her scalp because now it itched, and the urge to pull at the hair that was left was overwhelming.

"But you're upset."

She gripped the phone tighter. "And I'll be upset tomorrow about something else."

"Well, guess what. I haven't listened to you since this all started and I'm not going to listen to you now. I had meetings today, so I'm done early. I'm on my way," he said, and the phone line went dead.

True to his word, he was there within a half hour.

She heard his car and pulled open the door.

The moment he reached the door, he held out his arms, and she fell into them and sobbed. His hand rubbed small circles on her back. "What's wrong?"

She stepped back and looked at him. "Look at me. In that last two days it's all but completely fallen out."

"Sweetheart, it's okay." He wiped a tear from her cheek. "What do you want to do about it?"

"I'm going to just have to shave it off. What the hell else am I going to do?"

"I'll tell you what. Why don't we take care of it. I'll cut it off, and tomorrow we'll go buy you some wigs."

"A wig?"

"No, I said wigs." The crooked smile on his lips made her laugh, and she wrapped her arms around him as though it were the most natural thing to do.

When she stepped back and looked at him, the brown of his eyes had grown deeper, which was what happened when he was full of passion for something—or someone. Madeline bit back the joyful sob that lodged in her throat. "You've been planning this?"

"I was prepared for the day. I've looked up some shops that specialize in people who've lost their hair to cancer treatments. There are a million options, Maddie. If you want to feel good about yourself, there are people out there who want to help you, and I'm one of them."

She let out a sigh, and her heartbeat vibrated in her chest. It raced as it had when she was fifteen and looked at that face for the first time. He might be marrying someone else, but he loved her in his own special way, and that made it feel as though everything was going to be okay. "Thank you."

"Well, don't thank me yet. You might hate me when we're done. Are you ready?"

"For?"

"Let's do this. Let's cut off your hair."

CHAPTER 20

Madeline stared at her ex-husband, sucked in a breath, held it, and then dropped her shoulders as she let it out. It was time to let go of another part of her appearance. Really, with a flat chest, scarred and ugly, what did it matter if she had hair on her head or not? This was the next step. And if she was going to do something so drastic, there was no one in the world she wanted with her more than Carlos.

Carlos took her hand and gave it a squeeze, and they walked to the bathroom together.

"Where do you keep the clippers for Ed's hair?" he asked.

"Second drawer." She wrapped a towel around her neck and sat backward on the toilet seat.

He plugged in the clippers and took off the guard she kept on for doing the boys' hair. She took a deep breath and closed her eyes.

"Okay. Go."

He stood behind her with the clippers buzzing in his hand. "You're going to keep your eyes shut?"

"Yes, until I have a wig on my head."

"Chicken," he squawked and she shot her eyes open. "I knew that would do the trick."

He started at the top of her head. The clippers vibrated through her scalp. Madeline gritted her teeth to keep them from clattering. He drew them through her hair and ong strands fell to the floor.

"Oh, God!" Her lip quivered and she bit it to keep steady.

"If you cry, I'll carve my initials in it."

That made her laugh.

It only took a few passes, and her head was free of the dark hair that had graced her head since she was born.

She stared in the mirror that covered the length of the bathroom wall, no longer crying. It wasn't real. It wasn't her.

"I can't believe we just did that," she said, running her hand over the soft, tiny remnants of prickly hair on her head. "This is just crazy."

"You know what?" He smiled at her in the mirror. "You really don't look that bad."

The scars on her chest pained when he said that. Madeline smiled, looked in the mirror at how ridiculous she looked, and then looked back at Carlos and laughed. "What part?"

"Every part," he said, but he wasn't laughing.

Madeline swallowed hard. "Thank you."

"Okay, get up."

She stood up and brushed the loose hairs from her shoulders.

Carlos sat down and wrapped the towel around his shoulders. "My turn."

"Are you kidding me?" She laughed harder. Maybe he'd been drinking, but she wasn't gong to cut off his beautiful, thick, black handfuls of hair. "Stop. I'm fine."

"I'm not kidding." He turned and looked at her as he handed her the clippers. "Go."

"Carlos, I am not shaving your head."

"Fine. Then I'll do it." He took the clippers from her, turned them on, and made a pass down the middle of his head.

Madeline gasped and covered her mouth.

He examined the hairless patch in the mirror. "Now that really looks dumb."

"Oh my God, Carlos. What are you doing?" Her fingers shook at her lips as she watched him examine what he'd done. Astonishment swirled in her head, humor in her belly, and love in her heart for the man she should never have given away.

"Shaving my head because you won't."

Madeline dropped her hands and shook her head at him. "You shouldn't do this."

"Too late. If you're going to do it, so am I." He held the clippers up as if to hand them to her. "Now are you going to help me?"

She started with a giggle, looking at him. The realization of what he'd done and how silly he looked turned that into a full-blown laugh as she took the clippers from him. Timidly she took the first pass and watched as his dark, full hair fell to the ground.

Humor riddled her body and she shook from nerves and laughter as she made another pass and then another. Soon his head was as bald as hers, only with a dark shadow. When Carlos looked at himself and his shoulders bounced, Madeline laughed harder. They both looked hideous, and at the same time, she would never forget this moment.

"What are you doing?"

The laughter stopped as they both turned to see their children standing in the doorway.

A hiccup of a laugh busted through Madeline. She couldn't help herself. Their beautiful children stood before them, their mouths dropped open and their eyes wide.

Carlos ran his hand over her head. "Mom's hair fell out so I shaved it off."

"I got mad and shaved his off for spite," she joked and then laughed harder when the expressions on her children didn't change but only grew darker. "I'm kidding. He wanted me to do it." She placed her hand on his cheek. "He's being supportive."

"Fine." Eduardo shook his head, dropped his backpack, and walked past his parents and into the bathroom. Carlos stood up and he sat down on the toilet backward as his father had and pulled off his shirt. "I'm next."

"Oh, no you're not. You have the most beautiful hair, honey. Don't do this." She smiled. But when Carlos picked up the clippers and moved past her, she nearly choked on the gasp she sucked back. She wasn't quick enough to grab his hand and stop him. He turned them on and made the first pass right down the middle of Eduardo's head as he had with his own.

"Well, he's committed now. You'd better finish it off."

"Carlos!" She covered her mouth and tears formed in her eyes.

"It's hair, Mom. Finish it." Eduardo turned, took the clippers from his father, and handed them to her. "No one in this family does things alone."

Pride stopped her tears. The courage in his eyes and in the eyes of her ex-husband put the smile back on her lips. She took the clippers and began her attack on her son's gorgeous hair.

His smile was contagious and so was his laughter. She watched as large clumps of dark wavy hair, which matched his father's, fell to the ground and mixed with hers.

When they were done they cried, but not from pain, but from the joy of sharing an unforgettable moment, one that helped heal them all.

Madeline ran her hands over each of their heads. "I don't know that this is a good look for either of you."

"Funny enough, it looks pretty good on you, Mom."

"Your dad said that too." She looked up at Carlos.

"Okay." Carlos looked behind him at the two children who still stood in the doorway with their backpacks on and their faces white as sheets. "Clara, are you next?"

"Omigod! Dad! No!" she screamed as she ran down the hall.

"Chris?"

His grew wider and he fled down the hall following his sister, no words necessary.

"Real supportive." Carlos turned back with a smile and pulled both Madeline and Eduardo to him.

The strength that enveloped her sank into her body. She felt as if their love was healing her more than the drugs ever could.

CHAPTER 21

*C*arlos swept up the hair while Madeline helped the kids with their homework. He'd promised Kathy he'd have them all at the house by six for dinner with her parents, and now they were going to be late. He really had wanted to take Madeline shopping too, for something for her head, but that was going to have to wait.

He stood in the kitchen and watched his family work quietly on their studies. Madeline looked up at him. "I don't know if I can get used to you looking like that."

"It'll grow back fast." A pang of guild pierced his chest. His would grow back. Would hers? "For now maybe I won't look as old since all that gray is gone."

"What gray?"

"As if you hadn't noticed." He ran his hand over Eduardo's head. "We'd better get going. We're late."

The kids put their books in their backpacks.

"I'll come by"—he calculated his schedule—"Wednesday after school, and we'll go get you some fancy hair."

"I'll be fine." She touched his arm and gave him a smile that told him she appreciated what he had done. "Mom bought me some scarves when she was here. I think I'll try on a few and see what I think."

"If I know your mother, there are a few in there that are bright orange."

"Of course. They should accent my pasty skin very well, don't you think?"

Carlos shook his head. "Amazingly enough, you look great."

"Thank you for finding that amazing." Her words dripped with sarcasm, but the glint in her eye told him she appreciated his words. He could only hope she knew the sincerity of them in her heart. They hadn't been said to only ease her pains.

"Bye, Mom." Christian kissed her cheek with his eyes toward the floor.

"I love you," Clara said as she gave her a tight squeeze.

Eduardo kissed her cheek and then pulled her in tightly to his arms. "You're beautiful, Mom."

"Thank you, Son. What you did for me was amazing."

"What you're doing is amazing." He kissed her again and followed his brother and sister to the car.

"I'll call you tomorrow to check on you," Carlos said, stepping in closer to her.

"Thank you. You made something horrible into a precious memory. I can never thank you enough." She lifted her hand to his cheek.

He realized just how close he stood to her. There had never been any walls between them, except for the one they couldn't seem to hurdle when their marriage depended on it.

Her dark eyes gazed into his, and there was a peace within her. A peace he knew he was responsible for, and that warmed him to the core. He lowered his head and gently brushed her lips with his. She was soft, welcoming, and familiar. Her body swayed toward him. Instinct took over and he pressed his mouth harder to hers before retracting, realizing he'd overstepped a boundary he shouldn't have.

"I'll talk to you soon," he said quickly and retreated to the car. His heart still raced in his chest, and his lips tingled with the exhilaration of her kiss and the guilt of the moment.

"I can't believe you did that to your head," Clara was commenting to Eduardo when Carlos started the car. "You look like a dork."

"You look like a dork because you didn't do it," he retorted.

"Dad, why did you shave your head?" she asked.

"Why should mom be the only one without hair? It was making her really sad. It was the least I could do."

"It's called support, dweeb," Eduardo added.

"I think you both look goofy. Kathy is going to flip out."

Kathy. Any joy that had resonated through him from the special moments he'd created with Madeline became heavy in his chest when he thought about Kathy. He'd been so caught up in the moment with Madeline when he took the clippers to his head, he hadn't thought about Kathy.

Her parents' car was already parked in the driveway when they pulled in. There was a twisting in his gut. He wanted to back out of the driveway and just disappear for a few weeks until his hair grew back. Would she notice in her constant state of wedding planning? But the kids had already climbed out of the car and were headed up the steps to the back door.

He heard the shriek when she saw Eduardo.

Carlos cringed. What had he done?

"Ed, what did you do?" He could hear the shrill in her voice.

"Dad shaved mom's head, so I made her shave mine."

"He shaved your mother's head?" Her voice shook with the underlying tones of understanding, jealousy, and anger. But the anger prevailed as it hissed through what he knew were gritted teeth.

"All of her hair fell out," Clara added as she hung up her backpack.

"I can't believe you did that. What does your father think?"

"I took my cue from him," Ed said just as Carlos walked through the door.

"Oh my God!" Her voice stabbed him in the chest. "What in the hell did you do?"

Carlos swallowed hard. "I shaved off my hair."

"Why?"

"I was being supportive."

"It's horrible." The color in her cheeks rose, and he knew it wasn't just the hair. She was mad he'd gone to Madeline in a time of need.

"Thanks, dear," he said shutting the door and hanging up his coat on one of the pegs aligned on the wall. "Where are your parents?"

"They're in the living room, waiting for my family to get home and have dinner. You're late." Her voice had dropped into almost a whisper, but the tears forming in her eyes didn't diminish her disgust with what he'd done.

"I know. I'm sorry." He kissed her gently and held his lips to hers, wanting to make the pain of the kiss he'd laid on Madeline's lips go away.

She pushed against him and stepped away. "We are going to talk about this later."

"I know."

CHAPTER 22

*C*arlos passed by Kathy and headed toward the living room to welcome her parents. Perhaps if he made them feel welcome and happy to be in his home, he'd be less likely to be in trouble later, but he was sure that was still coming.

Her mother didn't have too much to say, which was amazing since the woman was a gossip. Her father, on the other hand, usually never spoke, but during dinner he had plenty to say. And the one thing he'd brought up was grandchildren. Grandchildren of his own.

He and Kathy hadn't even approached the subject of children. In fact, Carlos thought, he had his children. It had never been in his plans to have more. But when her father mentioned it, the hope on her face made his chest ache.

It was well past ten before her parents left.

Carlos turned off Christian's light. He'd fallen asleep in his clothes, he was so tired and Carlos left him.

He moved into Clara's room to tuck her in next.

"Will mom's hair grow back in?" Clara asked.

"I think so. When the cancer is gone for sure and they can let her stop taking her medication, it should come back."

"I think she looks funny."

"Don't tell her that."

"I won't." Clara snuggled into her sheets, and Carlos pulled them up around her chin. She reached up and grabbed his hand. "She's not going to die, is she?"

"Not until she's a very old woman."

"Thank you, Daddy, for taking care of her." Clara smiled up at him and then turned onto her side and closed her eyes.

Carlos sat there for a moment longer and then kissed her on the head.

Eduardo was looking in the mirror when Carlos made it to his door. He watched for a moment as he ran his hand over his head.

"Feels funny, doesn't it?"

"Yeah," his son said, still examining himself. "I have a scar on my head."

"You fell when you were about two. Cracked it on the coffee table."

"Coffee table? We didn't have a coffee table."

"Not after you cracked your head open on it."

Eduardo nodded. "This is going to take some getting used to."

"It'll be all grown back in before you know it."

He nodded, turning his head from side to side, examining it further in the mirror. "I'll keep it like this until all of Mom's grows back. That's only fair."

"That's mighty nice of you." He walked fully into the room. "I think it meant a lot to your mom."

"I want her to know she's not alone."

"I think she knows that." Carlos turned down the sheets on Eduardo's bed and sat down. "She's going to be okay. You know that, don't you?"

"Yeah, but I'm still freaked out. She's skinny, pale, bald," he said, throwing his hands in the air. "She looks so different." He shook his head. "I hope she doesn't notice when I stare at her because she looks like a stranger."

"I think she feels like a stranger."

"I just can't wait until she's all better. I don't like seeing her like this."

Tears threatened Carlos' voice. He took a moment to collect himself. Could a father be more proud of a teenage son? "I know. It's only been a few months. In a few more she'll be stronger. In a few more after that she'll be able to have reconstructive surgery, and that'll make her feel better."

"I just can't believe Matt left." He shook his head again and fell down onto the bed next to his father. "Why did he do that to her?"

So many reasons raced through Carlos' head. But the main one stuck. He wondered if Matt had ever really loved Madeline, or if he'd just taken her in as a sign to Carlos that he too could have what Carlos had. He'd always been that way when it had come to Carlos' family. "I don't know."

"But it's like she didn't even care anyway. I don't even think it upset her. She was more upset when we told her you were getting married."

The twisting in his gut was back. Just when everything should have been falling into place, it was falling apart.

"You'd better get some sleep. I love you."

"I love you too, Dad."

CHAPTER 23

$\mathcal{C}$arlos turned off the light and trudged toward his own room and the wrath he assumed was waiting for him.

Kathy was in the bathroom, and he could hear her going through her nightly ritual with a little more zeal than usual. Containers clanked and water ran on high. After a thud came a string of curses. She must've hit her hand on a drawer.

He undressed, slipped on his pajama bottoms, and climbed into bed waiting for her.

When she opened the door and stepped out, he saw it in her eyes. If he got any sleep he'd be lucky.

She didn't say a word, which was worse. She crawled into bed, turned off the lights, and pulled the covers up high.

Carlos lay sill in the silence of the room. She wasn't going to yell at him? She wasn't going to throw shoes? Maddie would at least have thrown her shoes at him.

He smiled at the thought.

Three black eyes, he remembered. Three. Maddie was a shoe thrower, and if you tried to intercept it, you'd get hit in the eye, because her aim sucked. It had taken him three times to learn it was always a better idea to stand still, you wouldn't get hit.

He rolled to his side and scooted closer to Kathy, wrapping his arm around her and kissing her on the head.

She snapped back the sheets and stood up. She glared down at Carlos as she turned on the light.

"Don't you get that close to me." She pulled the pillow from the bed, grabbed a quilt from the quilt rack, and bolted for the door. "I'll sleep on the damn couch."

"Kathy, wait." He scrambled from the sheets, threw his feet over the side of the bed, and nearly tripped as he hurried to her.

"Wait? Wait?" She dropped the pillow and quilt and stomped back toward the bed. "That's all I do is wait. I wait for you to call. I wait for you to come home. I'll be waiting for your Goddamned hair to be coming back in before we do the Goddamned pictures I had scheduled."

Carlos dropped his head. He'd forgotten about the pictures.

"Kathy, I'm sorry about the pictures. I forgot."

"You seem to forget a lot of things when it comes to me. At dinner the other night, I could have sworn you all forgot I was in the room."

He dropped his shoulders. "What does that mean?"

"It means you were all so damn concerned about her and so into watching her hold Tyler that you didn't even consider that I was there. You never took your eyes off of her." She tensed her arms as though looking for strength to keep going. And she did. "It was a reunion, and no one gave any thought to how I felt sitting there having you all talk about when you and Madeline were married. What Ed looked like when you brought him home. How young she was when she had him."

"Kathy…"

"You know we haven't even talked about having kids. You've never mentioned it."

"I have kids."

"But I don't. I'm thirty. I planned that when I got married to the man I loved, I would have kids."

"Then we'll talk about it. I just don't remember you ever mentioning it before tonight."

"You can't seem to remember a lot of things," she said again, as if the fight was starting all over. "You can't seem to remember that you asked me to marry you and we're planning a wedding. You don't care about colors, location, guests." She sucked in a breath. "I'm surprised when you can remember to drive to work in the morning."

"C'mon." He stood and walked toward her. "Listen, I'm sorry that I haven't been as attentive to you as I should be. I do remember that I asked you to marry me, and I wouldn't have if I didn't love you. And I said I was sorry about our hair and ruining your pictures. It'll grow back quickly."

"You look stupid."

"Really? I thought it wasn't too bad."

"Don't you joke with me. This isn't a joke!" She reached for the pillow again and Carlos stopped her, placing his hands on her arms.

"I know it's not a joke. We did it to support her. She was really upset about losing her hair."

"Damnit! That's all you do is support her! How about supporting me!"

"I do support you. I love you."

Her chest heaved with the breaths that came quickly as her anger rose. "I'm not so sure about that."

"I wouldn't say it if I didn't mean it."

Kathy lifted her head and pushed back her shoulders. Her eyes had grown dark and she seared him with their glare. "Then stop seeing Madeline."

It was as if the air had been sucked out of the room.

"I can't stop seeing her," he said, shaking his head.

"Why?"

"I have to see her. We share the kids."

Her lips tightened and she shook her head. "That's not what I mean, and you know it. I don't want you going by there everyday. I don't want you taking her to the doctor or taking her things from the drugstore. You don't need to be there."

"She needs me."

"She had her chance with you. You're mine now."

His jaw tensed. "Kathy, you're being petty."

Her eyes flew open and she pushed against his chest. "Petty? Petty?" She spun from him, dragging her fingers through her long, blonde hair. "I think I'm being pretty fair!"

He was never good at this part of the relationship. When a woman was in his face, he needed to recollect himself before he lost everything that was dear to him.

"You're right." He moved toward her again. "You've been nothing but kind and compassionate. I'm sorry."

"Then you'll stop seeing her?"

It squeezed at his heart. How could he possibly promise her that? "I need to support her."

"The kids support her. You don't need to be there all the time. Why the hell do you care so much?"

"She's my wife."

The moment the words were out of his mouth he'd wished he'd never spoken. He wished he'd just let her go to sleep and he'd never touched her.

Her hand came across his face.

"Bastard!"

"Kathy, I'm so sorry." The sting of the slap made his eyes water. "I didn't mean that."

"Yes, you did! You can't seem to get it through that thick, stupid head of yours. You divorced her! You asked me to marry you!"

Tears were streaming down her face. He wanted to gather her up and hold her tight. How could he have been so stupid?

"Kathy, I'm sorry."

"Are you having an affair with her?"

"What? No. Kathy, it's not like that."

She wrapped her arms around herself. "It feels like that."

"No. I'm just helping the mother of my children get through the hardest time of her life." He reached for her arms again. "Honey, I'm sorry this has hurt you."

She pulled back slightly. Her body shook under his hands. "It hurts so much."

"I never meant for it to. I love you."

"Then keep your distance from her." She turned and seared a look at him that made it perfectly clear the ultimatum if he didn't. "Please, do this for me."

He looked into Kathy's tear-filled eyes. He looked down at his chest. It felt as though she'd pushed a knife through his heart. How could he not take care of Maddie? How could he just walk away?

The thought of the kiss he'd shared with Madeline raced through his head. What was he doing? But he had to be honest with himself. He'd let Madeline go years ago. This was his chance to be the husband he should have been then. Carlos nodded. "Okay. I'll step back."

CHAPTER 24

*C*arlos' hand fidgeted over the phone as he sat at his desk. The students had long left the building, and his own kids were home waiting for him to arrive. But he couldn't move. He couldn't leave until he called Madeline and made sure she was all right.

A phone call wouldn't break his promise to Kathy. A phone call wouldn't hurt.

He finally dialed Madeline's number and waited for her to answer.

"Hello." Her voice was soft and gentle. That was Madeline. Soft and gentle.

"Maddie."

"Carlos!" Her voice rose, and he could hear her smile. "I almost didn't recognize myself this morning. I have to tell you. I laughed right out loud when I saw myself in the mirror."

Warmth spread through his body. "I'll bet you still look great."

"Thank you."

She was laughing. She was fine. He could hang up and know that she'd be okay.

"Hey, I just wanted to check on you. It doesn't look like I'm going to be able to make it to go shopping for a few days."

"Oh, that's okay. I'm getting this scarf thing down pretty well. They don't look too bad."

"Good." A lump formed in his throat.

"Arianna called me this morning. She's going to be here a few weeks between shows to throw your fiancée a bridal shower. She's got a few wigs from performances cluttering up her closet. She's going to bring them down for me."

"That's nice." His voice cracked and he swallowed that lump of raw emotion—deception for making the phone call—that had lodged in his throat.

"Carlos, is something wrong? You don't sound all right."

"No. I'm fine," he lied, and the palm of his hand sweated against the phone. "I've just got a lot on my plate and I'm trying to find time for it all."

"Well, if you'd stop fussing over me, you'd have more time," she offered.

He picked up a pencil that lay on his desk and snapped it in two with his thumb. "I'm not fussing."

"You're a good man, do you know that?"

He shook his head. He didn't feel like a good man, not when he was sneaking phone calls to his ex-wife when his fiancée asked him to keep clear of her.

"Call me if you need anything. I'll have the kids take the bus to your house on Monday, and they can stay with you next week."

"I miss them already. Isn't that crazy? It's not like they weren't here just yesterday."

"No, I understand it." He pinched the bridge of his nose. "I'll talk to you later."

He ended the call and dropped his head in his hands. God, he didn't know trying not to care for someone could be as hard as caring too much.

◠

KATHY HAD DECIDED TO GET MARRIED ON A SATURDAY MORNING IN April in the backyard of his sister's house among a small group of friends and family. It was February already, and Carlos knew that the eight weeks before the wedding were going to be a combat zone wrapped in pink.

"I need you to make me a list of people you want to invite. I think I know everyone, but just in case I miss someone." Kathy handed him a notebook and a pen.

"How many people are we going to be able to get into Regan's rose garden?" he asked as he looked at pages that she'd titled CARLOS' FRIENDS.

"I think we could get seventy-five people in there."

"Seventy-five?"

"Well, you have to think, with your family alone that's..." She began calculating. "That's twelve if you count spouses, dates, and kids."

"Not to mention my long list of dearest friends." He shook his head.

"Shut up and make your list." She gave him a wink as she went back about making her own list.

He couldn't help but think of the people he was putting on his list. It felt odd to put people down who had been there to see him marry Madeline. Most of them were relatives. He'd never kept too many friends. Matt Carson had been his closest friend in the world. He stood next to Curtis at the altar with him the day he married Madeline. He never would have guessed then he'd have lost his wife to the man he'd thought of as a brother.

Carlos shook his head. Sometimes you were blinded by friendship and love, and you never could see the wolf lurking in the person's clothing.

Matt had spent hours with him when problems with Madeline had begun. He had been his confidant, his sounding board, his strength. What kind of man takes that brotherhood and stabs you?

Matthew Carson, that's what kind of man. The same man who moved his way into Madeline's heart and convinced her to marry him only months after their divorce was final. Then five years later walked out on her when she needed him the most.

He let out a breath. Who needed friends when they were like Matt Carson?

They combined their lists. He had twenty. She had forty-three.

She looked up from his list, her brows drawn together. "Madeline isn't on your list."

"No. I left her off."

"Why?"

"Kathy, you can't tell me to leave her alone and then want me to have her there for the wedding."

She nodded as she stacked their lists together and paper clipped them.

"I want to tell you how sorry I am for being like that." Her delicate fingers crinkled the papers she nervously reclipped. "I've never been jealous before, and I don't like the way it makes me act."

Carlos pushed his chair back and crooked his finger for her to walk toward him. She stood and crossed to him, sitting on his lap just as he wanted her to do.

He wrapped his arms tightly around her. "You have a problem, do you know that?"

"What?" Her eyes narrowed again and her lips pursed.

"You're too nice."

"Quit," she said as she slapped his shoulder.

"Do you know what she would have done in your situation?"

Her lips tightened. "What?"

"She would have thrown a shoe at my head." Kathy laughed but quickly reeled it back in. Carlos pulled her closer to him.

"Really. She gave me three black eyes in the ten years we were married."

"I don't believe you."

"Okay, I ducked from the shoes and ended up moving right into their line of fire, but that's my story."

Her shoulders hunched and she cuddled into his chest like a small child. "You're a lucky man to have a relationship with your ex-wife like you do."

"I know that. I also know I'm a lucky man to have a woman who loves me and wants to marry me."

"Thanks." She brushed his lips with a gentle kiss. "She's fortunate to have had you around. I'm sorry that I ruined that."

Carlos shook his head. "She'll be just fine without me meddling in her day-to-day affairs. She's an amazingly strong woman with a great will to live and do many wonderful things."

Kathy sat up on his lap, cupped his face in her hands, and kissed him again. She lingered for a moment, and Carlos knew she'd fight that jealousy demon for a long time to come, but she was trying. What more could he ask for? She gave his cheek a playful pat, which he thought might have been just a bit too hard, and then stood and went about tiding up the kitchen.

Carlos sat and thought about what he'd said. He was right about Madeline. She'd be fine and she'd go on and make a life for herself. Sooner or later the kids would be grown and they'd have no reason, except weddings and births, to even see each other.

The thought struck him as hard as the shoes she'd once thrown at him. He didn't want that. Madeline had been a daily part of his life since he was fifteen. How could he give that up?

CHAPTER 25

*K*athy pushed through the rack of dresses she had chosen. There were eight. With Regan and Arianna's help, she'd been able to eliminate five of them.

"I like the simple elegance of that one." Arianna pointed to the dress Kathy held in her hand with its straight skirt and scooped neck. "It's just simple and elegant."

"That would encompass the statement simple elegance." Regan laughed at her sister.

"You know this is all beyond me. If you weren't going to appreciate my opinion, why did you ask me to come?"

"I appreciate your opinion," Kathy said softly. "I'll try this one on first." She walked toward the dressing room with the dress that Arianna liked best. As she undressed she could hear the banter between her future sisters-in-law.

"So when are you getting married?" Regan's voice was muffled through the door.

"Right. I see that happening in the near future," Arianna was quick to quip.

"Giving up?"

"No. I'm just too busy to care. Besides, everyone in my

industry is so adept at telling lies for a living, I think they forget which ones they've already told me."

Regan laughed. "In time."

"Well, I'm thirty-eight years old. I don't see myself settling down now and starting a family. I'll just have to spoil Tyler."

"Zach's already talking about having more."

Kathy paused with the dress over her head. Was it wrong to hope that Reagan would hold off on another baby until she had convinced Carlos to have one? Was it wrong to want, for once, some of the limelight?

Arianna huffed out a loud breath. "Tyler is only three months old. What's the rush?"

"Oh, I think we'll start trying at the end of the year. I want him to have siblings that are close in age like we were."

"Yeah, Mom and Dad had their hands full for a while. I think about the time I was ten, you and Carlos were both eight, and Curtis was six. How did Mom keep her sanity?"

"She's a saint."

"No kidding."

Kathy slid the dress down her body and emerged from the dressing room. Both Regan and Arianna stood, their mouths dropped open in awe.

"Kathy, its gorgeous," Reagan said as she laid her hand to her chest. Her eyes filled with tears, and when Arianna noticed she nudged her.

"Having a baby has made you sappy." She walked toward Kathy. "It's just beautiful."

Kathy looked in the mirror. "Do you think so?"

"This is your wedding day. You're supposed to have whatever you want."

Kathy nodded. "Maybe I should show it to Carlos."

"Are you kidding me? The man has no taste. You can't show it to him until you walk down the aisle. Those are the rules." Arianna settled her fists on her hips.

"You sure are an expert," Regan added, nudging her sister back.

"Well, I've seen enough of these things. I've seen simple and I've seen yours. Your six-hundred-person wedding with more flowers than a flower shop."

"We didn't have six hundred people."

"Felt like it."

"You're jealous."

"As if." Arianna shook her head and turned her attention back to Kathy. "Try on the other two. Let's see what they look like."

Kathy retreated back into the dressing room with another dress. She wished her own sisters had been able to be there with her, but they lived too far way to make the trip more than once. She missed her family and wished she had the kind of relationship with her sisters that Arianna and Regan shared. All of the Keller siblings looked out for each other. Even Curtis, who was the baby, wasn't treated like one. She was the baby too, and wasn't she always reminded?

She slid on the dress of white silk and let it fall over her curves. Looking at her cleavage, full and beautiful in the bodice of the dress, she thought of Madeline. She sighed.

What would it be like to be going through what she was going through alone? Was she scared of dying or had she come to grips with it all? It had been months since she'd had surgery and started her chemotherapy. Had her hair grown back like Carlos'and Eduardo's? Was she feeling any better than the last time Kathy'd heard Carlos talk about her? Clara mentioned that she was going to have more surgery to get her boobs back, as she'd put it. Was that going to be more painful than having them removed?

Kathy touched her hand to her chest. She'd been so unfair to Carlos in asking him to not have anything to do with Madeline. It had been three weeks, and he'd been home every night. He'd been attentive. He helped pick out invitations and gave his opinion on flowers. He took his brothers to the tux rental store and they had initial measurements done. Everything she needed from him, he'd given, without argument and without one mention of Madeline's name.

Kathy felt ill. She'd said she was going to see Madeline since the day they'd found out she was sick. She'd never made it to her door. It was time.

When she walked out of the dressing room, Regan and Arianna shook their heads.

"You like the slimmer one better?" Kathy asked, and they both nodded. "I think I do too."

She turned and looked at herself in the mirror. She wasn't feeling like a blushing bride at the moment. She was feeling like a grinch.

CHAPTER 26

*K*athy stood on the doorstep of the house that Madeline and Carlos had once shared. Carlos had the kids, and she knew Madeline should be home from work. She'd lied and said she had a late meeting and wouldn't be home until late. She thought it was a bit ironic that when it came to Madeline, neither she nor Carlos could be completely honest with each other.

She'd picked up a bouquet at the florist and wondered if the gesture would seem silly. Letting out a breath and rang the doorbell.

When the door opened, Kathy almost didn't recognize the woman who stood before her. Madeline was in a business suit with high heels, a suit coat, and a beautiful white silk blouse. But it was the deep red hair that brushed her shoulders in a swingy bob that had thrown her off.

"Kathy," Madeline said, her voice rising in obvious surprise at finding Kathy standing on her doorstep. "Is everything okay?"

"Yes, everything is fine." She tried to keep her voice even but found it extremely hard to do. "I've been meaning to come by for a visit."

"Well, come in. I'm sorry, I didn't mean to leave you out in the cold." Madeline opened the door and Kathy stepped through. "I just got home from work. Make yourself comfortable. I'm going to change my clothes, and I just made some coffee. I'll bring us out some. Do you take anything in it?"

"No, black is fine."

"I'll be right back."

She'd never been inside the house. She'd been outside when Carlos had dropped off or picked up the kids from time to time. It was a simple design from the outside. A house once picked out by a young couple with the mindset that they would fill it with family. Inside it was homey. A candle burned on the mantel of the fireplace. A quilt had been thrown on the back of the couch as if someone had recently stood from under its comfort. Pictures of the kids she cherished were everywhere.

Their current school pictures were set on the mantel in big elegant frames. The same pictures hung on the walls of Kathy's home, but she only now noticed that the children's clothes matched in color and accented the colors in the room.

She laid the flowers on the coffee table and looked at the other collages of pictures. They were filled with Madeline and her children, all of them at varied ages. Eduardo's first bike was red, and Clara had curly hair as a baby. Christian played baseball, and when Eduardo graduated from kindergarten, Madeline wore her hair long and straight.

Kathy swallowed hard. She stared at the wall in front of her, plastered with its eclectic mix of photos, and realized that was what she wanted. She wanted a matching wall with pictures of children she gave birth to.

She felt lightheaded and sat down on the couch.

None of the pictures had Carlos or Matt in them. Madeline had done her best to remove the men from her life.

One frame across the room caught her eye. It had three slots on it and was tucked behind the lamp. The photos were small, but in each one of them, there was a family. The first picture was of a newborn Eduardo nestled in a hospital blanket between the adoring faces of his mother and father. Next the same pose with Christian and next with Clara. Tears stung her eyes. Carlos was so young then and so handsome. But the hardest part was seeing the love in his eyes. He wasn't even looking at the babies or Madeline in the pictures, but it was there. It was deep inside of him. Her lip quivered. He'd never looked at her like that.

"Sorry to keep you waiting," Madeline said as she entered the room with two cups of coffee and set them on the table. She'd changed into a pair of sweatpants and a baggy T-shirt. Her head was now wrapped in a bright orange scarf, and her feet were covered in fuzzy pink socks.

Kathy readjusted her position on the couch to better see Madeline as she sat across from her. "I should have called. I'm so sorry."

"No, not at all. This is nice."

Madeline's eyes were soft, and Kathy knew she sincerely meant it. Clara's eyes looked the same when she gave compliments, which Kathy realized for a young girl, she did often.

She picked up the flowers she'd brought for Madeline and handed them to her. "These are for you."

"Thank you. That was thoughtful of you." She smelled them and smiled.

"I was just admiring the pictures of the kids."

"They're growing up so fast. Everyday Ed gives me a countdown until he can drive." She shook her head as she laid down the flowers and picked up her cup of coffee. "I'm not sure I'm ready for that."

"I don't think his father is either."

"It's funny. Regan and I are the same age. My kids are ready to drive, and hers is learning to hold his own bottle. All big milestones."

Kathy sipped her coffee and hoped Madeline didn't notice her hands shaking.

"How are you feeling?"

"I'm doing better. It's nice to have a little energy again. I still have a long road, but I feel much better."

"Clara says you're going back in for surgery soon."

"Yeah. I'll have reconstruction done at the end of the month." Madeline's eyes clouded over, her shoulders stiffened. "I'm scared as hell."

"Why?"

"I've just have read too much." She rolled the tension from her shoulders and then tucked her feet up under her. "You know having your breasts removed sucks, you anticipate the hard times to come. Getting them back should be the easy part, but it's not."

"Let me know if I can do anything for you."

"I'll be fine, but thank you."

The brush-off hurt, but she didn't know what else she'd expected Madeline to say. The few minutes she'd been there suddenly felt like hours. Kathy set the coffee mug back down on the table and picked up her purse. "I should be getting home. I promised everyone I'd bring home something for dinner. But I wanted to bring this by for you." She reached into her purse and pulled out a wedding invitation.

"Thank you," Madeline said as she reached for it, and Kathy noticed her hands shook too.

"I just wanted you to know how important you are to everyone and that it wouldn't be the same without you there to share this day with us."

Madeline bit down on her lip. "Are you sure? This is your special day, and I don't want to intrude on it."

"I'm sure," she said as she stood. "I'm glad you're feeling better."

"Thank you. Thank you for coming by."

Kathy nodded and moved toward the door. "By the way, I really liked the red hair."

Madeline laughed. "Did you? Arianna brought it for me. It's been fun. I have six wigs in all different colors and lengths. It's like being someone new every day."

Kathy clutched her purse under her arm tightly. "Call us if you need anything."

Madeline nodded. "Thank you."

CHAPTER 27

*K*athy walked through the back door of the house with her arms full of bags. She'd driven around for an hour before she finally stopped at the grocery store and picked up sub sandwiches and chips. Carlos jumped up from his chair and helped her with the groceries.

"This wasn't the takeout I thought you'd bring." He crinkled up his nose.

"I just couldn't come up with anything better," she said as she shrugged off her coat and hung it on the hook.

The kids picked up their books and papers, and Carlos walked back toward her after setting down the bags.

"Are you all right?" he whispered as he touched her arm.

"I'm okay."

"Did something happen?"

"Nothing bad. Let's talk about it later, okay?"

Carlos nodded and went about cutting up the sandwiches and opening bags of chips.

When everyone had settled in for the night, Carlos found her in the living room with a magazine on her lap, looking out the window into the darkness.

"Hey, what's up?" He sat down next to her on the couch, and she adjusted until she was wrapped in his arms.

"I wasn't at a meeting tonight," she admitted and felt his body stiffen. "I went to Madeline's house."

He didn't respond right away. When he did he asked, "Is everything all right?"

Kathy nodded her head. "I just haven't been dealing well with the way I acted a few weeks ago. I've never been a jealous person before." She turned so she could look him in the eye. "I never had anything to lose before."

"You're not going to lose me."

"But I think I was threatened that I didn't have all of you."

His brows knit together in obvious confusion. "What do you mean?"

"I've never needed you in the way that she has. You shared something with her that I've never shared with anyone. You were in love when you were young. I was still searching. You've seen your children born and looked at their mother like she was the most perfect person in the world. I'm still waiting for that day. You have a friend in her that I don't have with anyone I know." She sighed and a tear fell. "When I was trying on dresses with your sisters, I realized that your family is so amazing. I don't have the kind of relationship your sisters have with my own sisters. Yours don't even live nearby, and yet they're still so close you wouldn't know they only speak on the phone a few times a week."

He sat quietly and let her talk. "When I was at Madeline's, she had pictures all over of her and the kids. It was like nothing I'd ever seen. My mother only ever kept up our school pictures." He gave her a gentle squeeze as if to tell her he understood what she saw. "But what got me were three little pictures hidden behind a lamp."

"Newborn pictures," he said simply.

"Yeah, newborn pictures."

He nodded and kissed the top of her head. "Is that what bothered you? Pictures of me in her house?"

"Maybe a little."

"Why were you there?"

Kathy turned again to look at him. Her stomach tightened. "I took her an invitation to the wedding."

He gave her a slow nod, and the crease between his brows deepened. "Why did you do that?"

"Because she should have been on your list. You should have had her on your invitation list, and because I was being childish, she wasn't there."

"It's okay. She's my ex-wife. Most ex-wives don't attend the wedding of their ex-husbands."

"But the two of you are different." She wiped at her eyes. "When I was trying on dresses, I was looking at myself. I realized everything she had gone through in the past few months. Except for the kids, you were all she had. I took that away from her in her time of need because of my own selfishness. I had to change that. I can't be the bad person I was feeling I was."

His mouth softened into a smile, but the crease between his brows didn't lessen. "I don't think you have it in you to be a bad person."

"She's going to have surgery again at the end of February."

"Clara and Ed mentioned that."

When he said it like that, she knew he'd completely stepped away from Madeline, just as she had asked him to.

"I want you to be there for it." Her voice was finally unwavering. It finally felt good to encourage him to take care of Madeline. "I want you to be there when they take her in and while she's in recovery."

"Kathy, don't do this."

"No. You need to be her support. She needs you. Please."

Carlos kept his eyes on her and his face softened. He bit down on his lip and began to slowly nod his head. "Okay. I'll call her and get the details."

"Thank you."

"Come here." He stood and pulled her hand. "I wasn't going to show this to you until Valentine's Day, but I think I want you to see it now."

He led her to their bedroom and shut the door. She sat on the bed, and he walked to the dresser. He pulled an envelope from his sock drawer and turned toward her.

"I took my mother shopping the other day. When we couldn't find anything, we called in reinforcements. So Regan and Arianna met us. Can I tell you it was the longest day of my life?" He laughed and she shook her head, not understanding him at all. "Anyway, when I couldn't find what I wanted, and the women in my life hadn't been any help, I called your mother for some insight."

"Insight? Into what?"

He sat down next to her and opened the envelope. "Your ring." He pulled a familiar ring out of the envelope, and Kathy's lips quivered.

"Carlos, that's my great-grandmother's wedding ring."

"I know. I'm glad I called your mom. She said you'd always had your eye on it."

"It was like no other ring," she said, smiling at the princess-cut ruby set in rose gold.

"She asked me to give it to you. She wanted it to be your wedding ring."

She lifted her hand to her lips to stop them from trembling.

Carlos examined the ring he held between his fingers. "If you want to wear it as your wedding ring, we'll put it on your left hand. If you just want to keep it and have me get you another one, we'll put it on your right."

Kathy stuck out her left hand and Carlos slid the ring onto her finger.

He was going to marry her. In his heart he loved her. But when he looked at her and smiled, she wondered when the love he had in his heart would reach his eyes.

CHAPTER 28

*M*adeline laid the necessary items she'd need for her hospital stay on the bed. One by one she checked them off her list as she put them into the suitcase.

The next time she put things into a suitcase she was going somewhere far, far away and warm. A beach. An ocean. A margarita!

Clara stood at the doorway and watched her mother's process. "So will you look normal when you get done?"

"Don't I look normal now?" Madeline asked with a smile.

"You know what I mean."

"I do, and I'll still look different. But I think I'll feel better about myself."

"What are they going to do?"

Madeline decided it was a good time to sit her down and explain the procedure. Besides, maybe she could instill in her eleven-year-old daughter the importance of taking care of herself. Especially since she noticed Clara's breasts were starting to fill in.

"Come here." Madeline walked to the large overstuffed chair in the corner of the bedroom and sat down. She patted the seat next to her, and Clara climbed up. She reached across to the nightstand and grabbed the pamphlet that she'd studied over and over again. "This little book tells you all about what the surgery is going to be like."

Clara took it and flipped through the pages. "This sounds gross."

"I suppose it is."

Clara crinkled up her nose and looked at Madeline. "They're going to cut your stomach and take off the skin?"

Madeline only nodded, but she wanted to laugh. Clara was right. It sounded gross.

"They have to take the skin from somewhere to rebuild the breast."

Clara flipped though a few more pages. "Will you be"—she grew quiet—"as big as you were?" she whispered.

"I've opted for a smaller size."

Clara lifted the pamphlet. "Why do this?"

"It's just a personal thing, honey. I want to feel normal again."

"You don't feel normal?"

"No, baby. I don't." She touched her cheek to the top of Clara's head.

"Why?"

"Well. . ." She gave it a moment's thought. "It's been hard. I didn't know if I would die or not. I'm lucky. They have medications and procedures that make women strong, and we survive things like this. I had to have surgery to remove my breasts so they could take out the cancer. I lost my hair and got very sick from the medication that kept the cancer away. Now I have a little hair, and I can have surgery to have some of my body back. Maybe by next year it'll be like nothing ever changed."

"Will they look the same?"

"No. They'll never look the same again. But that's okay. I don't need working breasts." She smiled and Clara scrunched up her face.

"Working breasts?"

"Yes, I won't ever be feeding a baby again, like Auntie Regan does."

"Oh." She focused back on the pamphlet. "So you won't have those?" She pointed to a picture of a nipple.

"I could have that done, but I don't think I will." She swallowed hard. Never before would she have thought something like a nipple would be important to consider. "But who knows, I might change my mind."

Clara snuggled closer to her. "I'm glad you're feeling better, Mom. I was scared."

"You know what, honey?" She smoothed her daughter's hair with her hand. "So was I."

"Maybe when you feel better about yourself, you'll get married again."

Her heart ached when she thought about marriage. "Maybe I will, but I'm not too interested in that right now."

THE DAY OF HER SURGERY, MADELINE PULLED INTO THE DRIVEWAY of Carlos' house. The sun hadn't risen yet, and the kids were still in their pajamas. They reluctantly climbed out of the car and walked up the back steps to the house.

The kitchen light was on, and Madeline got out of the car and watched as they walked inside. She saw Kathy in the window and she waved. She was glad the kids had stayed with her for the night.

"Today's the day." Carlos stepped out of the house and stood on the step with a cup of coffee in his hand.

He was shaven and dressed for the day. She smiled up at him. It had been so long since she'd seen or talked to him. All of his hair had grown back in, and he was as handsome as ever.

She suppressed the stirring in her stomach. "Yeah. In a couple of days I'll look normal again."

"Couple of days?"

"My doctor says I can probably go home in two days."

His lips tightened, and she noticed his eyes shift to her body. "Good." He disappeared back into the house.

Madeline shook her head. That had been more awkward than she'd expected. He'd stopped talking to her and coming by almost four weeks ago; why she thought he'd have a full conversation with her was beyond her. She opened her car door and caught sight of him though the kitchen window kissing his fiancée. Kathy smiled up at him, and Madeline watched him pull his coat from the hook and open the back door. She climbed into her car, not wanting to draw out a moment that had obviously made him uncomfortable, but he ran around the side of her car and knocked on her window.

Madeline let out a breath. She didn't want to talk to him, she wanted to drive away, quickly. Instead, she rolled down the window.

Carlos zipped up his coat. "Park it over there." He pointed to the side of the driveway. "We'll take my car."

"What?" Her attitude had taken a nosedive after watching him kiss Kathy as though he knew he was on display.

"I'm taking you to the hospital and staying with you."

"Carlos, don't be…"

"Park it, Maddie!" He smiled with a wink of his eye, and she sat staring at him. What was she supposed to do? First he's in her face wanting to help her, then he just disappears. Now there he's standing here grinning at her telling her he's taking her to the hospital? Once she was done with the surgery on her breasts, maybe she could get a lobotomy so she could forget how much the man could twist her insides up.

She reluctantly moved her car to the area where he'd pointed, turned it off, and climbed out. By the time her feet hit the ground, he had her bag out of the backseat and the garage door open. She looked up at the window where Kathy still stood looking out at them. She waved, but the smile on her lips was forced. Madeline knew she might be supportive, but it didn't mean she was comfortable with Carlos' decision to take care of her.

Madeline followed him toward the garage. "What's going on?"

"I already told you," he said as he walked toward his car.

"No." She grabbed his arm, stopping him from putting the bag in the backseat. "You were in my face from the minute Curtis called you and told you I was at the hospital, and then one day you stopped calling. I haven't seen you in four weeks. Now here you are telling me what to do. Telling me that you're going to take care of me again? I don't need your charity, Carlos Keller."

The dimple in his cheek deepened. "Then think of it as Kathy's charity, because she's the one who told me I had to take care of you again. Now get in the damn car or you're going to be late."

Madeline huffed out a breath and trudged around the other side of the car. She climbed in and fastened her seat belt. As Carlos backed out of the garage, she looked up at the back porch. Her children stood there in the pajamas. Kathy stood in a robe with a cup of coffee. They all smiled and waved, and the kids blew kisses. Tears fell from her eyes as Carlos turned the car out of the drive and proceeded to the hospital.

"Thank you," she finally said as they turned onto the highway.

"For what?"

She let her shoulders drop. There was no need for tension when she was with Carlos. "For caring."

"Well, I'm going to say this, and then I'm going to hate myself for it, but I would have been there for the past four weeks had it been up to me."

"Kathy?" She should have known. Carlos never would have just drifted away from her.

"Yeah, Kathy." He signaled to change lanes, checked the mirrors, and then glided into the center lane and picked up speed. "She found she had a new emotion. Jealousy. She hates herself for it, but it's understandable."

"I've kinda put a damper on her perfect wedding."

He shook his head. "No, she's still having the time of her life putting it together."

Madeline twisted her fingers together. Carlos' eyes shifted to her and she set her hands flat on her lap. She knew he was waiting for her to process her thoughts. There was a time they could have a conversation without words. Though she didn't think they'd strayed too far from that. Madeline turned to watch him. "She came by the other day and saw me."

He made another lane change. "She told me."

"Did you know she was going to do that?" she asked, straightening her fingers and trying to relax.

"No. She told me she had a meeting. I had no idea."

Madeline nodded. She wanted to hate the woman, but it was just impossible to do.

Carlos shifted a quick glance her way. "You are going to come to the wedding, aren't you?"

"I don't know. I just don't think it would be right."

He shook his head. "I'd like you to be there." He reached for her hand and gave it a squeeze.

How could she tell him she wasn't sure if she could do it? She couldn't stand the thought of him marrying someone else. Watching him say I do to someone else just might literally break her heart. But then again she deserved it. Karma was a bitch.

CHAPTER 29

*M*adeline checked into the hospital. She was in a room having her vitals taken by six o'clock.

The sun was rising outside her window. She'd never paid much attention to little details like sunrises or sunsets until she got sick. Now it was a habit to watch the sun come up just to make sure it did.

Carlos walked back into her room. "Okay, they say you'll be going in about eight o'clock." He packed up the few items she'd taken out of her small suitcase and zipped it up.

"Okay."

He moved to her side and took her hand. "I'll be here."

"Thank you, Carlos. Thank you for everything."

"My pleasure, honey. Hey, I also found something in the hallway. I thought you might like it." He moved to the door.

She sat up straighter. He still called her by the pet names he'd called her when they were married. Oh, how she wished it didn't make her heart rate kick up when he slipped them into conversation. "Really? What?"

The moment he opened the door, Madeline gasped and

163

covered her mouth with her hands. One by one his family walked through the door.

"You weren't going to sneak in this time." Curtis crossed to her took her hand.

Alan and Emily walked to her side next. Emily kissed her on the cheek and whispered to her in German. Madeline didn't know what it was she said, but she knew it was a prayer.

"I can't believe they wouldn't let you wear your hair." Arianna moved to her side. "I hear you're a knockout in the red one."

"It's my favorite," she said, smiling up at her.

Regan pushed through the rest of them and hugged her tight. "I hate that they wouldn't let me bring Tyler in for you to see him. Zach said he'd text a picture when he got him up and dressed. So you'll be able to virtually see him when you wake up."

"You're going to be here when I wake up?" Her voice cracked from the tears that stung her throat.

"We all are," Regan promised, and all heads nodded.

They all stayed in her room until it was time for her to head to surgery. That kept her calm, but when the nurse told them they'd have to leave, Madeline's heartbeat kicked up and her palms grew damp.

Only Carlos stayed behind and walked next to her as they pushed her down the hall on her bed.

He held her hand, rubbing his thumb over her knuckles. "You're going to do great." He leaned in close to her.

"I can't believe your whole family is here." She'd always belonged more to the Kellers than she did to her own family. Her mother had called the day before to say good luck, but her sisters hadn't said a word.

"You're family. You will always be a part of our family."

There was no reason to hold back the tears that were induced by his sentiment. "Thank you."

When they reached the door to the operating room, Carlos

lifted her hand to his lips and brushed them with a kiss. "I'll be here when you're done."

"Promise?"

"Promise." He leaned in and pressed his lips to hers and laid a warm, soft kiss on her mouth.

Madeline took his hand and gave it a squeeze. Love and compassion for the man at her side swirled inside her. She had to say what was in her heart. "Hey," she said looking up into his dark eyes. "I love you," she said, figuring she had nothing to lose.

As they pushed her through the door, she closed her eyes so she couldn't see his reaction.

CARLOS FELT LIKE HE'D SWALLOWED A BOX OF OLD-FASHIONED chalkboard erasers. He couldn't get her words out of his mind. During the first hour of her surgery, his family kept giving him sorrowful looks. He mustn't be containing his emotions very well.

She'd meant them as a term of endearment. Of course she loved him. They were friends and he was taking care of her. They'd loved each other since they were fifteen. They just hadn't been able to function as a married couple.

That had to be the part he kept in his head. They couldn't be married. It hadn't worked out. Things were just too hard for them to be married. But they could always love each other as friends.

Carlos pressed his hands to his face. What had been the breaking point? Who had said it was over? He didn't know. But for years he'd lived with the fact that Madeline was Matt's wife. He'd searched for a woman he could love with all his heart, other than Madeline. He'd finally found that woman in Kathy.

What had Madeline really meant when she said she loved him?

Without a word, he walked out of the waiting room, but

Arianna was hot on his heels. By the time he sat down in the small chapel, she sat right next to him.

They were silent for a long time. He'd expected some kind of lecture, but she didn't say anything.

He stared at the cross that hung from the ceiling in front of the stained-glass window. "She told me she loves me."

Arianna nodded. "Did you ever doubt that?"

"I must have doubted it five years ago."

She took her brother's hand. "You are so supportive of her. She's always going to love you for that."

"I should have been more supportive when she was my wife. I was so focused on finishing school and going on in my career, I think I forgot what was important. God, she worked two jobs, took care of the kids, and supported everything I did. What did I do? I kept going to school and was mostly unemployed."

"But you can't blame yourself. That was what you both agreed on."

"Yeah, and somewhere I lost that, and Matt picked it up. He took care of her. I didn't do that. I didn't give her the chance to enjoy her children or participate in school events. I didn't take care of her."

"You're doing it now."

"Now, when it's too late."

Arianna shook her head. "Why is it too late?"

He turned his head toward her and rolled his eyes. "I'm getting married in four weeks. All she ever wanted me to do was move on. I finally did."

"The dress is gorgeous, by the way," she added, nudging him and smiling. "But there are still four weeks for you to really process what you're feeling."

"I'm just having wedding jitters." He patted his sister's hand and breathed in her calm to settle his nervous stomach. "I'm also just worried about someone I care deeply about."

"I'll always be around if you need someone to talk to." She

gave his hand a squeeze. "Even when I'm in New York, I'm always around."

"Thanks."

"By the way, I'm staying with Maddie for the next few days, and while Zach is out of town, Regan and Tyler will be staying with her."

He smiled. "You guys have this all figured out?"

"She's part of our family. We all care for her. We always have and we always will." She settled her eyes on his. "Kathy is even making dinners for her for the next week and freezing them. No one is leaving her behind."

"I don't think she knew how lucky she was."

"Too bad. We should have all been here for the first surgery."

Anger still swarmed inside him when he thought about the phone call he'd received from Curtis that morning. "Yes, we should have."

CHAPTER 30

*C*arlos was right next to her when the pain in her chest forced her to open her eyes. This time she'd expected him to be there and would have been disappointed had he not been.

"Hi," she said weakly as she gritted her teeth against the pain in her chest.

"Hi." He kissed the fingers of the hand he held in his. "How are you feeling?"

"Like shit." She tried to laugh, but it hurt.

"They're planning on keeping you at least overnight until they're sure the grafted areas are okay and so is your reconstruction."

She tried to look down, but she was too stiff. Her chest was covered in bandages and cold compresses. Again, tubes darted from the bandages for drainage.

Madeline let her head sink into the pillows. "Did I tell you I was going on vacation?"

"Yes, the last time you decided to have surgery."

"No, no." She smiled and turned her head to him. "I decided that when this is all over I'm taking a vacation. I'm going somewhere warm where there's a beach and water and margaritas."

His eyebrows drew together. She knew he wasn't comfortable with her traveling, but she knew she had to get away. But he forced a smile. "I think that sounds wonderful."

"Me too." She closed her eyes and sighed. "I'm tired of working so hard and never playing. Besides, after all of this, I think I deserve it."

"Oh, honey, you deserved it a long time ago. I really should have done those things for you." There were those sweet words again. How could she let him marry someone else when he called her honey and sat by her side in the hospital?

"Well, things are different now, aren't they?"

"Yeah, they are."

She kept her eyes closed, not wanting to look into his. "I may need to have the kids back for a few weeks. They say I'm going to be unable to lift my arms for a while."

"My family already has that planned out."

She opened her eyes and shifted them to see him

He smiled. "Arianna is spending a few nights with you when they release you, and then next week when Zach goes out of town Regan and Tyler are coming to stay."

Her heart swelled with the love she had for his family. "Oh, that is so wonderful."

"And," he said as he kissed her fingers again, "Kathy is making meals for you. She's freezing them so you'll be able to prepare them easily."

Her eyes watered. "I don't deserve that."

"No one deserves it more."

She sucked in a deep breath and swallowed back the fear that was boiling in her belly. She needed to address the last thing she'd said to him before she went into surgery. "I want to say I'm sorry for what I said earlier."

"Don't you dare apologize for that."

"I'm just very emotional and very appreciative of everything you've done for me."

A nurse entered the room to take her vitals. "I'm going to check her bandages and tubes. If you don't mind stepping out for a few minutes."

Carlos nodded. "I'll go let everyone know you're doing well and give the kids a call."

"Thank you, Carlos, again. For everything."

He gave her a smile as he left the room.

Madeline rested her head against the pillow as the nurse pulled back her gown. The cold air hit her sharply just as the emotion had when Carlos had enlisted his family to be there for her. She closed her eyes as the nurse checked the drainage tubes. It would be nice if, just like the reconstruction to her chest, her relationship with Carlos could be mended. But they'd severed that that relationship as much as the surgeons had when they removed the cancer from her body.

She'd been given a second chance at life, and even if she couldn't have a second chance with Carlos, she could still have those little moments between them.

MADELINE'S FREEZER WAS FULL OF FOOD. HER HOUSE WAS FULL OF flowers and cards. And Arianna brought her a cup of tea every hour to keep her warm.

"Thank you," she said with her teeth chattering.

"Are you sure you don't want to take the cold packs off?"

"It just feels so much better with them on. I'd rather be cold." She tried to lift the half-filled mug to her lips, but every slight movement caused pain. She took a little sip, and set it down in her lap. "I can't wait until this is all done."

"Do you think it was worth it?"

"Asking me that now isn't fair." She chuckled and winced

from the pain. "When I see myself in a real bra or a low-cut shirt, I'll have a better answer for you. Right now, no. It wasn't worth it."

Arianna nodded. "Carlos said you want to go on vacation when you're done with it all."

"Yes. Somewhere warm. I guess that'll be the real time to ask me that question. If I look good in a bathing suit, then yes, it will have been worth it."

"You know. I was thinking of doing that very same thing as soon as my next production is over. I have a tiny little nest egg that would hold me over."

"Oh, yeah? Where were you thinking?"

"Cancun."

"Oh, that sounds nice." The very thought warmed her. She'd never been out of the country. In fact, the only travels she'd ever had were on her honeymoon with Carlos, for which they drove to New Orleans; and they'd gone with Matt to see Arianna in New York when she debuted on Broadway; and they took a trip to Las Vegas. She thought it was time she experienced something more than work, motherhood, and being a breast cancer survivor.

Arianna lifted her mug to her lips and watched her over the top of it. "I was thinking maybe we could plan to go together."

"Oh, that would be fun."

"I think so too." Arianna sipped and lowered her drink. "I went that one time with, oh what was his name?" She tapped her finger to her lips as she processed the thought.

"Gavin."

"Oh, my gosh. How do you remember that?"

"Because it was just about the time we got married. Carlos didn't like him at all."

Arianna laughed. "You know what, I didn't like him either. But he was paying my way to Mexico." She kicked her feet up on the coffee table and leaned her head back on the chair. "Did I ever tell you he asked me to marry him?"

"He did?" Madeline laughed and then winced again from the pain. She readjusted, hoping to ease the discomfort.

"Yeah. I don't think he was serious though. At least I didn't when I snorted wine through my nose when he asked."

"Was he mad?"

"Oh, hell yeah. I never saw him again."

Madeline moved the cold compresses and sipped her tea, which was already tepid. "Are you seeing anyone now?"

"Me? Nah. I just don't have time. No one in New York does it for me."

Arianna always was more of a country boy sort of girl. Madeline was sure she didn't find too many Southern boys in New York. "That's too bad."

Arianna shrugged and tossed her hair over her shoulders. "No big deal. Some of us just aren't made for marriage."

"Yeah, I guess we're not," Madeline agreed, feeling let down that she'd struck out twice.

"Zach has already told me I have a date to the wedding. Do you know John Forrester?"

"John? Yeah, I think I've met him. Foreman for Zach's company, right?"

"Yeah. Carlos used to work under him when Regan started with his company."

"That's right," she shifted on the couch and Arianna stood to adjust her pillows. "Well, Zach has decided that would keep us both out of trouble."

"How considerate."

"Sure. He's twenty years older than I am, and I guess he's been though a nasty divorce. Sounds like a beautiful night."

"You'll make the most of it."

"You bet your ass I will. Of course, I get the elder divorcé and my brother gets the French heiress."

"Simone is coming to the wedding?"

"Only because she'll be in town. Her father's company is building some monstrosity in Louisiana, and of course they're going to use Zach's company. She's doing most of the footwork on it. I think it just keeps her from spending Daddy's money on lavish un-necessities."

"I can't even imagine." There hadn't been anything in Madeline's life that hadn't been of complete necessity in years. That too was going to change.

CHAPTER 31

Three days with Arianna at the house had been more like a slumber party. By the time Regan arrived, there were dishes piled in the sink and unopened mail strung all over the kitchen table.

Regan squeezed a decent amount of dish soap into the sink and ran the water to fill it "You know when I lived in my sister's house, she would have killed me if I had left a mess like this."

"Yeah, I'm not much help," Madeline said as she sat at the cluttered table for the first time since her surgery.

She'd done away with the cold compresses, but she continued her pain medication religiously. She could lift a teacup to her mouth, or as the case was, lower her head to the cup, but she still couldn't lift her arms far enough to wash her face. Arianna had helped her do that, and now Regan was there to do the same.

Regan turned from the filling sink and began to throw away the trash that her sister had strewn about.

Madeline watched her with amusement as Regan picked up after her sister. "Where is Zach's meeting?"

"Louisiana. He's building a corporate headquarter building for Pierpont Oil."

"Arianna told me that Simone was in town overseeing the process."

Regan laughed. "Yeah, if you could call it that."

"Not very business oriented?"

"Have you never met the woman?" Madeline shook her head. "I love her. I absolutely adore her. She has filled my closet with the most wonderful shoes and designer looks. But a mind for business—" she stopped and raised her brows with a shake of her head. "I don't know what her father is thinking."

"Maybe he's trying to give her some responsibility."

"If Zach wasn't making more on this build than any other in the history of Benson, Benson, and Hart, I don't think he'd do it. She's a face among the investors, that's it. He's doing all the work."

"Her father knew that would be the case?"

"I think so."

Regan turned off the water in the sink and began to load the dishwasher with the dishes that didn't need a good soak. Madeline watched Tyler enjoy his swing. He wasn't a fussy baby, not like Eduardo had been. She was glad she'd been young enough to have the energy to take care of him then. He'd certainly outgrown the fussiness and learned to fuss over everyone else. She knew someday he'd make a great husband and father.

"Did Simone go with Zach to Louisiana?"

Regan loaded glasses into the washer. "Yep."

"And that doesn't bother you?" Madeline was sure she'd heard enough about the woman to know she was a French beauty and a very playful one at that.

"No. She's been chasing my husband since they were seven. He's never shown interest in all these years, I don't see him changing his mind. Besides, she finds a new sailor in every port, if you know what I mean. I'm sure she'll show her face for the cause, and Zach will handle the business."

"I've heard she's Curtis' date for the wedding."

"Yeah. It'll keep them both out of trouble."

"Or get them into it," Madeline said with a smile, and Regan returned it with laughter.

But Regan's laughter died down as she filled the soap dispenser of the dishwasher. She shut the door, turned to Madeline, and leaned against the counter. "Are you going to be there?"

"No." Her answer was definite. She didn't want to see the man she loved marry someone else.

Regan's brows knit. "Why?"

"It's just not right for me to go. Kathy certainly doesn't need me there. This is her special day."

"And Carlos is okay with that?"

Madeline chewed the inside of her cheek. "No. Kathy personally brought me an invitation, and Carlos told me he wanted me there. Regan, I just don't think I can do it." She would have liked to pick up the sleeping baby from the swing and hold him close to comfort herself, but she couldn't hold anything heavier than her cup of tea. She adjusted in her chair for comfort and to hide her emotions from Regan. "I know he spent the last five years watching me share my life with another man. I'm just having a really hard time watching him move on. But on the other hand, it's about damn time."

Regan walked to the table and sat down across from Madeline. "Aside from you, he couldn't have done better."

The thought should have brought her some comfort, but instead her heart ached. She wondered when things had gone so wrong for them so long ago. He shouldn't have to be moving on at all. Madeline should have always been the better choice. Why had they decided they weren't good for each other? It was certainly too late now, wasn't it?

CHAPTER 32

$\mathcal{C}$arlos drove down the street where he'd lived with Madeline years ago. There was still a pain that pierced his chest, knowing he'd only be driving away to head to another home.

For now, he'd take the time he had and visit with his ex-wife and his kids, and be grateful that he'd escaped his own house, which had been draped in pink by his sisters for Kathy's bridal shower. But in the backseat, Tyler slept in his carrier. Carlos had been given the important task of babysitting so that Regan could keep some sanity about her, and dry boobs, he'd been reminded.

He pulled up in front of Madeline's house and smiled when he saw his boys in the driveway playing basketball.

"Hey, Dad!" Christian waved. "Wanna shoot some hoops?"

"Maybe in just a bit," he answered as he ducked back into the car and unbuckled Tyler's car seat from the backseat.

"Oh, you're the babysitter today?" Christian held the ball under his arm as he walked closer to the car to peek at the baby. "Hey, Cuz, what's up?" Tyler smiled and Christian nudged his father's arm. "Hey did you see that? He smiled at me."

"I think it's just gas."

"Funny, Dad." He went back to shooting the ball at the hoop as Eduardo helped Carlos with the diaper bag.

"I think he looks just like Aunt Regan."

"I think so too. But don't tell Audrey that. She thinks he looks just like Zach."

"Everyone has an opinion," he laughed as he opened the door for his dad. "How come you brought him here?"

"I needed to be absent from the party, and I thought your mom would enjoy seeing him."

"I think that will make her day."

The sight of Madeline sitting on the couch, her feet tucked under her, and not one compress in sight warmed him. Her white cotton T-shirt had a scooped neck, and he could see the proud swell of her breasts. Obviously, by the choice in her clothing, she was pleased with the results.

Different levels of excitement ran though his body. Of course he was as happy about her having new breasts as she'd seemed to be by letting them peek through her shirt. But there was always that side to him that still got stirred up at just the sight of her, and not just her chest.

It had been four weeks since her surgery and he knew, from talking to the kids, that she was finally getting back the mobility in her arms.

She was wearing a bright orange scarf on her head, and he was pretty sure she had on makeup.

Carlos walked into the living room and set the baby carrier down. "I brought you a visitor, I hope you don't mind."

"Oh my goodness," she said, moving quickly toward the baby. "Look how big he's already gotten."

"Mom, do you think he looks just like Zach?" Eduardo asked as his father unbuckled him from the seat and picked him up.

"Not one bit. He looks just like Regan."

"That's what I think."

Carlos held him to his shoulder, adjusted him, and turned to Madeline. "Do you think you can hold him?"

"I'd love to try. Will you sit right next to us in case I need you?"

It all seemed so familiar. They'd shared a moment like this once, but it'd been their own baby they'd cradled and admired. He let his emotions settle before he spoke. "Of course."

Madeline held out her arms and Carlos laid Tyler in them gently. He then slid up right next to her, placing his arm around her shoulders, keeping a hand on Tyler for support.

Carlos watched his children all filter into the room. Clara didn't move toward Tyler as she normally would. Eduardo and Christian stood back, and they all just watched.

He looked back down at Tyler, who was awake and smiling up at Madeline, holding tight to her finger. The look on Madeline's face was priceless, and he knew they all saw the same thing. She looked like she was glowing.

The color in her skin was almost back to normal. The smile on her lips was radiant. The optimism in the room was infectious. He realized, aside from his precious nephew, it was just his family in the room. His children and their mother and him. Peace filled the room. Madeline had tilted her head and rested it against his, and his hand rested gently on her shoulder. Never had he felt with such comfort with anyone else, not like he did with Madeline. That thought hit him. But there was someone else. There was Kathy—and while he was sharing moments with his ex-wife, Kathy was celebrating their future.

When Tyler became fussy, Carlos reached for him. "I'll take him."

"Oh, please don't. He's just hungry. Perhaps you could make him a bottle."

Carlos rose from the couch and went to make Tyler's bottle. He was glad he had a reason to release Madeline from his arms and get his thoughts in order.

He wasn't surprised to find step-by-step instructions in the bag. Regan, even though she wasn't officially an executive assistant anymore, she kept everyone around her organized and on track.

Carlos made Tyler a bottle and then resumed his position next to Madeline so she could feed him. But this time he left some space between them.

She took the bottle and set it to Tyler's lips. "Thank you for bringing him. This is wonderful. I needed this."

"I thought it would be good for you."

"Look at my face," she said, turning to him. "Do you notice anything?"

She turned her face from side to side and smiled.

It took him a few moments of contemplation. "Your eyebrows grew back."

"Yes!" She smiled wider. "Isn't that wonderful?"

"You look great. You really do."

"I feel great. At my last appointment they said my blood work looked good. My cell count is back up and normal, and there are no signs of cancer."

"So you're in remission?"

"They won't say it until I finish my treatment next month, but yeah, it looks like maybe I am."

"You did great." He kissed her on the cheek instinctively.

He felt her suck in a breath, but she kept her eyes on the baby in her arms.

LUNCH HADN'T SETTLED WITH CARLOS. THE FOOD WAS FINE—IT was the whole conversation. No, he didn't want a bachelor party. He didn't need to go out and live up the single life one more night. He'd never been a fan of the single life. Curtis seemed to be the only person who needed to live on the wild side once in a while. Sooner or later, Carlos thought, his brother was going to get caught by something wild, and it would want to tame him. Wouldn't he be in for a shock?

Things at home just hadn't been right. They hadn't been any different either, he realized. He was preoccupied. Kathy seemed distant. Even the kids seemed just tossed back and forth between them all.

He was used to it happening when it came to the kids at school. Once spring hit, no one could concentrate. But the fact that it was happening in his own home, with his wife to be, and himself, was throwing him off.

He just needed to relax. Everything would be just fine.

But even he couldn't make himself believe his own lie.

CHAPTER 33

Kathy had opened sheet sets, china, and appliances. Everything she had registered for was set before her in a beautiful display of boxes, with bags of discarded wrapping paper and bows set next to the pile. She was glad Regan had wanted to have her shower at her own house, and then she wouldn't have to transport everything home.

She'd been right about Judy's gift of the condo. It would be a nice way to spend her honeymoon in Hawaii with her new husband.

It was surreal. In just three more weeks she would be married to Carlos. She looked around the house with its mountain of boxes and trays of leftover food. If the shower had been that much fun, she couldn't wait until the wedding.

Carlos had hurried into his office the moment he'd returned home. Regan had kicked him out of the house so fast, he hadn't had time to finish his grading. He wasn't one who liked to get behind on that, so he wanted to get the grades in the computer before dinner.

Tyler had fallen asleep again, and by the look on Regan's face, a stranger would have thought she'd been weeks since she'd last seen her son. She'd hurried out the door with him to get home before he woke.

The house was quiet, and Kathy sat down on the couch and kicked her feet up. So many things still needed to be done in the three weeks before the wedding. There was one more meeting with the photographer, a finalization on the cake, and they still needed to pick out a song for their first dance. Audrey Benson had taken care of the caterer after Kathy had given her a list of items she wanted them to have; that was at least the one thing she knew she wouldn't have to think about again.

The dresses had arrived at the bridal store, and they would have a final fitting for them the next week. Regan was still trying to get the perfect body, even though Kathy and Arianna had told her repeatedly she looked wonderful.

The invitations had all gone out and RSVPs were pouring in. They'd had very few nos. The afternoon wedding looked to be as perfect as she'd always dreamed it would be.

She looked again at all the gifts that filled the room and let out a long breath. If everything seemed to be going just right, why did she feel so unsure about it all?

Each day when she woke, she felt a little more uneasy. She just couldn't pinpoint why. She loved Carlos and adored his children. His family was nothing but wonderful, and even his ex-wife was easy to get along with and she considered her a friend. Why then couldn't she shake the feeling that something just wasn't right?

She hadn't told Carlos, but her body had felt so strange, she'd even taken a pregnancy test. It was negative, but she was only looking for answers. She wanted a baby, but not until after they were married and had planned it. The doctor had told her she was stressed, but besides that, she was healthy. What more could she ask for?

Wedding jitters, she figured. Everyone had them.

∾

CARLOS WATCHED CURTIS, IN HIS GREEN SCRUBS, AS HE WAVED TO A nurse across the diner then slid into the booth next to him. "Oh, my brother, you are going to love us!"

Carlos shook his head. "You know those words alone scare the hell out of me."

"Don't worry. I've got your back," Zach ensured him.

"And I've got his," John Forrester ensured him further.

"Thanks." Carlos grunted.

Curtis leaned over the table. "Why doesn't anyone trust me?"

Zach laughed a hearty laugh as he leaned back against the booth. "Oh, I don't know. Because John had to carry me home after my party and Regan almost killed me, him, and you."

"And me," Carlos added. "And I don't even think I was there."

"Oh, you were there. You just ducked out at bedtime."

"Well some of us have families to think about," he reminded him.

"That's right," Zach added. "So don't get me killed this time."

"Well I don't have that problem. So I'm not going to worry too much about it." Curtis waved at the waitress to take their orders. "Tell me about my date, Zach."

The waitress took their orders, and Curtis focused in on Zach.

Zach shrugged his shoulders. "Tell you what? You've met her."

"Right. Sexy French girl who came to your wedding with a date who was what, twenty?"

Zach nodded. "Yep, that's her. She's a little more mature now."

"Too bad," Curtis sipped his water and wrinkled his nose at Zach. "Maybe her dad will let us use the yacht for our party, since he was lenient enough to let you use it for your honeymoon."

"Let's focus, shall we?" Zach returned his attention to Carlos. "Are you okay with all of this?"

Carlos rearranged his silverware on the table. "A bachelor party? Sure. I'm game."

"How about we just all meet up at a sports bar and throw back a few," Zach offered.

Curtis shook his head. "You're all getting soft on me."

"Yeah, sounds great." Carlos scratched his head then looked out the window.

"Do you even want to do this?" Zach asked softly.

He turned his attention back to the table. "I'm all for it."

"Won't be like the first one. Man, you were smashed." Curtis leaned his arms on the table.

"So were you, and you were underage. We could have gotten arrested."

"You know, I work seventy hours a week. I save lives. I think I deserve a little release."

The other three men at the table shook their heads at the most educated man among them. "You're right. When you get married, we'll go all out," Zach promised.

"Great."

Soon the topic of bachelor parties past and future were forgotten, and meals of greasy hamburgers and french fries were consumed. Zach bragged about Tyler. Curtis gave too many details about a date with a cute resident. John talked about the inspection he was going to head off to, and Carlos sat quietly.

John finished first. He handed Zach a wad of folded-up dollar bills and shook the hands of the other men at the table. "I guess I'll see you all in a few weeks, then."

"It'll be interesting to see which one of us ends up with the better date." Curtis grinned.

"Well said, in this company. I promise to treat mine like a lady and have the most respect for her the next morning." He winked at Zach.

Carlos and Curtis both narrowed their eyes at John in reaction to his comment about their sister, and Zach laughed. "I'm kidding. I've met her. She's a very nice lady. We'll have a nice day together." He waved his hand. "See ya'll later."

"Funny guy," Curtis told Zach.

"John—he's harmless."

A moment later Curtis was excusing himself and following a group of nurses out the door. Carlos shook his head as he watched his brother amuse the women with his charm.

"So, are you going to give it to me straight?" Zach scooted closer to the center of the booth. "You really don't want a party, do you?"

"Oh, that's fine. I could use a night out with the guys."

Zach nodded. "So is everything set and ready for the wedding?"

"I think so. I'm not allowed too close to the bridal bible," he scoffed. "But I think we have almost everything set."

"Regan is so excited she can hardly see straight. She hasn't entertained since Tyler was born."

"Kids take a lot outta you."

"They sure do. I wish I could help her out more with the house and Tyler, but I have so much work."

"Work will always be there. Just stay under her radar. Pick your socks up off the floor. Load and unload the dishwasher. And never believe her when she just says the word fine."

Zach gave him a slow nod. "I'm glad I have you to set me straight."

"Well, I wish I would have had the knowledge up front."

"Kathy's lucky that you've been trained."

Carlos reached for his wallet and settled up his part of the bill. He wasn't comforted by the thought that being trained meant that he'd screwed up the first time. Had he flown under Madeline's radar, maybe he wouldn't be getting married for a second time, he'd still be married to Madeline.

Zach reached for his water. "Are you guys going to have kids too?"

Carlos shrugged. "She's mentioned it. Her parents have

mentioned it. I guess we'll see what happens. What about you guys?" He quickly changed the subject.

Zach took a drink. "Oh, yeah. She wants them close together. So I suppose we'll start trying when Tyler is about a year old. Does that sound about right?"

"Don't ask me. My kids just kinda happened."

"Yeah. Too much thought takes all the fun out of it."

"I suppose." Carlos looked at his watch. "Well, I should be heading out."

"I'll call you and let you know what the plans are."

"Thanks." He shook his brother-in-law's hand and headed out of the diner.

CHAPTER 34

The way Madeline looked at it, there was no time like the present. Her boss had offered her vacation time, and she thought she should use it wisely. There was never a good side to having cancer, unless your boss had gone through it and knew when you deserved to celebrate your remission.

Carlos' wedding was in less than two weeks, and she really didn't want to be there.

That wasn't true. She did want to be there, but she didn't want to be a guest.

She blew out a breath. At what point were her feelings for him going to go away? She deserved to watch him get married and be happy. He'd watched her marriage for years. Only truth was, she hadn't been happy.

Madeline searched the travel website for the best deal. She was headed to Cancun, without Arianna, though maybe they'd take that trip some other time. For now, she just needed sun, and it needed to be as far away from Carlos Keller as possible.

Twenty minutes later, she had booked her flight and printed her itinerary. Now all she had to do was dig out her passport. She and Matt had gotten passports two years earlier. It was on a whim. They didn't even have plans to go anywhere.

She opened her closet and found the firebox that held all her important papers. Inside were the birth certificates of her children, social security cards, and of course the unused passports of both her and Matt. She'd have to send him his.

Deeper into the box she found her marriage license to Matt. She took it out of the box and crinkled it into a ball. What a worthless piece of paper that was. She let out a growl of frustration and opened the ball of paper and flattened it out.

Further in the box, she found a manila envelope that contained the final documents from her marriage to Carlos.

She shook her head. What an unhappy box. Unused passports and forfeited marriage licenses. When she sat the metal box down on the floor to look in the envelope, she heard a clanking noise. She knelt down to take a look and noticed Carlos' wedding band loose at the bottom of the box.

She fell to her knees on the carpet and took out the ring. It wasn't fancy. A small, round, piece of gold was all he'd worn to symbolize their unity. She held it to her chest. She'd been twenty years old when she bought that piece of metal. Twenty years old, and she'd known what she wanted more than anything. No matter how angry they were at each other, they'd never taken their rings off until the day the papers had arrived saying their marriage was obsolete.

She slipped it on her middle finger. It was much too big. She wondered if he'd like to have it. Then again, maybe Eduardo or Christian would like it. She stood and walked to her dresser; atop of it stood a wooden jewelry cabinet. She opened it and took out a chain. She'd wear it around her neck and when she thought about it, or if someone asked about it, she would make her decision on who would get to keep it.

She felt the weight of the gold on her neck as she went about gathering suitcases and other items she could pack for her trip. No time like the present to get packed.

The shuffling of several pairs of feet walking through the front door caught her attention. She'd have the kids the week before the wedding. She was supposed to have them the week after too, while Carlos and Kathy were on their honeymoon. How come she hadn't thought of that? She'd booked her trip to miss the wedding, but hadn't thought about being needed for the kids while they were on their honeymoon. She'd see if maybe Arianna would stay with them. If she was already heading home maybe she could intrude on Regan, though she didn't want to do that. It would be too far for her to drive them to school every day.

How come it always happened that the moment she'd done the first selfish thing for herself in almost fifteen years, the guilt was taking over. Her family needed her and she was escaping. Madeline shook it away. No. She was leaving and she was going to enjoy herself. Her kids were old enough not to be a burden to anyone. It was going to be fine—she hoped.

"Hey, Mom." they all shouted as they passed her on their way to the kitchen.

The thought that she wouldn't see them for a week, or talk to them either, squeezed her heart. She was going to miss them so much. "Hey, guys. How was school?"

"Boring," Christian was quick to answer.

"Maggie invited me over for a sleepover this weekend. Can I go?" Clara asked.

"We'll have to see." She moved up behind Eduardo and gave his head a rub. His hair had come back in, but it was curlier than it had been. "How are you today?"

"Fine." He grabbed a bottle of water and a banana and headed to his room.

Unable to resist, she followed him.

"You doing okay?" She leaned on the doorjamb and watched as he situated himself into his room.

"I'm fine."

"Okay, if you say so." She watched him. He looked so much like his father. She gave it another moment and then turned to leave.

"Mom," he called, and she turned with a smile. He opened his banana and took a bite. "Do you remember Tasha?"

"The girl in choir that you wanted to ask to homecoming?"

"Yeah, that's her."

She remembered that she was two years older, a junior, and he'd had eyes for her since he started high school.

Eduardo rubbed the back of his neck with his hand. "Well, she asked me to prom."

"Really?" Her voice rose as she spoke. "Well, that's good, right?"

"Sure. But I can't drive her. Doesn't that seem stupid?"

"Not if you don't have a license, it doesn't."

"I really want to go."

"Doesn't she drive?"

"Yeah, but I want to do this right. And don't get me wrong, I don't want you or Dad to drive us either."

Madeline gave a shrug of her shoulders. "I can understand that."

He set the banana on his desk and dropped his shoulders. His eyes were bright, and she knew his head spun with a million thoughts. Eduardo rubbed his hands on his pants and looked up at her. "But what do you think if I asked Uncle Zach if he'd let us use his company's limo. I'd pay for it," he was quick to add.

"How do you suppose you'd do that?"

"Well, I was thinking maybe I could work for it." He sat on his bed; the Tennessee Titans bedspread reminded her that he was still her little boy, while the man inside of him fought for new freedoms.

He bit down on his lip. "You know I'd like to be an architect after I graduate from college." She nodded, pleased he'd added the bit about college. "Well, I was thinking maybe Uncle Zach would let me work at his place for a few hours after school, and I could just learn stuff. I could also help out around the office. Like an intern. I know I can't touch much, but what do you think if I ask?"

She blew out a breath. "I guess it can't hurt to ask."

"Thanks, Mom."

"Sure." She turned to walk away. "You know, he does have a new build not too far from school. And I'm sure John Forrester is overseeing it in some way. Your dad used to work for him."

"I remember John, sure."

"Maybe you could work on site too. That would give you some hands-on."

"Wow, that would be really cool."

"Should I field this for you? Do you want me to talk to Aunt Regan first?"

He smiled his big toothy grin. "How did you know?"

"I've been around you a long time."

"Thanks, Mom. By the way, you look really good today."

"I have on my red hair." She gave the wig a little flip with her hand.

"I like the red hair."

"So do I," she said. "Oh, and I wanted to tell you I'm taking a vacation in a couple of weeks. I'm going to Mexico. I'm going to ask Auntie Arianna to stay with you."

"Okay." He shrugged. "Why can't we just stay with Dad?"

"Well." She tried to keep her voice upbeat. "I decided to go while they were on their honeymoon. It's not too thought out, but my boss gave me time and I thought I should do it while I could."

"Sounds great, Mom. You deserve a vacation in a swimsuit."

"Dear, God! I hadn't thought about a swimsuit."

His shoulders bounced as he laughed at her, and his eyes grew bright. "You're going to Mexico and you didn't think about that?"

"No. I just wanted to get away for a bit. Well…" She blew out a breath. "I guess I'll be thinking about it now." She looked down at her chest and placed her hands on her breasts. "Damn glad I have these."

"Mom!" Eduardo turned and covered his eyes, forcing her to laugh.

CHAPTER 35

$\mathcal{A}$s soon as she left his bedroom, she went right to hers and picked up the phone. First, she'd call Arianna and see if she could fill in while she was gone.

"You're going to Mexico without me?" Though she was trying to sound put out, she didn't have Madeline convinced.

"Now is just the time for me to go."

"Okay, okay." She laughed. "We'll plan a weekend though. Don't you think we should all get away? You, me, and Regan. Just like old times."

Just like old times. It used to be sisters. They were all sisters. They'd known each other since high school, and every year they would spend a weekend away, just the three of them. Then after she divorced their brother, they took off for a few years. Especially when Regan was in Hawaii and Arianna had moved to New York. But eventually, one thing had lead to another, and they'd had three more weekends. Even Matt had thought it was good for them to get away together.

She felt it coming and she knew she had to ask. "What about Kathy?"

"What about her?"

"Well don't you think we should include her? Or you should take her, is what I guess I really mean," which it was.

"I had never given it any thought," Arianna said, her words drawn out. "Wow, that makes me a bad sister-in-law, doesn't it?"

"Well, no…"

"Yes, it does. Dear God! Here we are helping her plan this wedding and making sure her dress is right, she has the right accessories, and dancers for her bachelorette party, and I don't even think to include her in sisters' weekends."

"It always takes getting used to," Madeline added, trying to move the subject along, sadness swelling in her chest at the thought of the years she'd lost with her dear friends.

"No, it doesn't. I never had to get used to you," she said and then laughed. "I mean, you were always around."

They'd all grown up together, in a sense. That busy time in life when Arianna was seventeen and Madeline, Carlos, and Regan were fifteen, they'd all been a unit. She was their sister and the love of Carlos' life. They had all been used to each other, and even ending her marriage to their brother hadn't stopped their relationship.

"Well, I won't feel put out when you all jaunt off to Mexico for a vacation."

"Oh, Maddie, shut up!" She erupted in laughter on the end of the phone. "You know you've always been one of my best friends, and Regan's too for that matter. Just because Carlos was too stupid to hold on to you doesn't mean I have to let you go."

Madeline smiled one of those smiles that make your cheeks hurt. "Thank you. From the bottom of my heart, thank you."

"Anyway, you need me to stay with the kids?"

"Yeah. Carlos and Kathy will be on their honeymoon. It just worked out that way."

"Sure it did," she said, not quite under her breath. "I'd love to stay. Can I just stay out at your house?"

"Yes, that would be perfect."

She had her tickets, her hotel room, and a babysitter. All she needed to do now was try and get her son a job. She shook her head as she dialed Regan's number. Who would have thought the time would come she'd be helping her son move into his adult life and pay for dates with girls?

"I will definitely talk to Zach about it," Regan said once Madeline told her about Eduardo's plan. "Have him call him tomorrow about two thirty. That's when he's the least busy."

"I guess you would know best. You were his favorite assistant," Madeline teased.

"Yes, but I got fired."

"But in the end I do think you got the best job of all."

"You couldn't be more right. So... are you coming to the wedding?"

Madeline let out a sigh. "That's another reason I'm calling. I need to borrow a swimsuit."

"You're coming to the wedding in a swimsuit?"

"No, no, no." She laughed again. God, she loved Carlos' sisters. "I'm not going to the wedding. I'm going to Mexico. Arianna is going to watch the kids while I'm away."

"Why? He's looking forward to having you there."

"And I'm flattered, but Regan, between you and me, I can't watch him do this. It's already breaking my heart."

"I knew that," she said softly. "What timing, eh?"

"Yeah, what timing." She took another deep breath. "So I'm a coward with a boss who gave me extra vacation time, even after having been on leave. I'm taking it. So what do you say? Do you have something sexy I could wear to show off my nipple-less breasts?"

She was glad she'd called her ex-sisters-in-law. She felt better than she'd felt in months.

Now, all she needed to do was get out of town before Carlos said I do, and she'd spend the next week sipping margaritas on a beach and not have to think about the wedding at all.

CHAPTER 36

*M*adeline's phone rang at ten o'clock at night. She reached across the bed to the end table to pick it up. When she looked at the caller ID and saw Carlos' number, a surge of panic raced through her, but it quickly diminished when she realized why he must be calling. She'd expected him to call earlier in the day. Regan and Arianna were usually much quicker about spreading gossip.

"You're not coming to my wedding?" Carlos demanded without even responding to her hello.

Madeline pushed her shoulders back, ready to stand her ground. "No, Carlos. I'm not."

"Why?"

Did he really need an answer to that question? Hadn't she been fool enough to tell him she loved him when they wheeled her into surgery? She sighed. There was her proof that he either hadn't heard it... or had heard it but accepted it as a friendly gesture.

"My boss gave me vacation time. After all I've been through, I just think this would be a nice reward for myself."

"And you couldn't have gone a week later?"

Madeline gripped the phone tighter. "If you're upset because I asked your sister to stay with the kids…"

"No. That is not why I'm upset." He let out a breath. "Maddie, it's important to me to have you at the wedding."

"Carlos, did it ever occur to you I don't want to watch you move on?" She tensed. She hadn't wanted to say that to him, but now it was out.

"You'd rather I be miserable the rest of my life."

She slouched down on the bed, her back resting on the backboard, causing her scars to stretch and become as uncomfortable as the stirring in her stomach from Carlos' disappointment. "Now, I didn't say that."

"It was okay for you to go get married six months after our marriage ended? It was okay for you to marry my best friend? But now, five years later, I can't marry a perfectly wonderful woman, who adores you by the way, and be happy?"

Her heart ached as he replayed her mistakes since they'd divorced. "Carlos, I want you to be happy."

"You just don't want to be a part of it?"

Why was he arguing about this with her? She was his ex-wife. That alone should be reason to not have to justify why she wasn't going to attend the wedding.

She didn't want to tell him that his taking care of her had put her at such ease, and now he was all she thought about. She didn't want to tell him that when she drifted to sleep each night, she dreamed of him. How could she tell him she loved him as much at that moment as she had when she was fifteen? Only when she was fifteen, there was hope. Now there was just emptiness. She'd never have him again as her husband. She'd walked away from that, and now Kathy had it. They'd always be parents and share their family, but he was marrying Kathy—and it broke her heart.

How was she supposed to tell him that? Instead, awkward silence took over the phone call.

Carlos let out a deep breath. "I just wish you'd change your mind. That's all."

"I only want the best for you, Carlos. That's all I've ever wanted." That much was true. She'd hoped when they'd committed to each other that nothing could break them down so badly that one of them would walk away. Now they both had.

"I know." His voice dropped off. "You're one of my very best friends. I can't imagine not having your blessing on that day."

"You have my blessing."

"And I'm thankful for that." He let out a weak cough, and she knew it was strained with tears. "I'll see you when you drop off the kids."

"Okay, oh, did you hear that Zach has a new intern?"

"Of course I did. Ed's excited and it'll be good training for him. Maybe it'll help him get some scholarships, and if he's got potential, Zach can let us know."

She felt better ending the call on a lighter note. "Well, I'd better get to bed. I'll see you in a few days."

"Night, Maddie."

She lay down across her bed and fingered the circle of gold that still hung around her neck, between her new breasts.

"Let go, Maddie," she told herself as she moved Carlos' ring back and forth on the chain. "Let go."

As if Madeline's phone conversation the night before with Carlos wasn't unsettling enough, Matt called the next day.

He cleared his throat. "I just wanted to see how you were feeling."

"Really? How nice of you to check in on me five months later. Did you wonder if I was terminal yet?"

"Madeline…"

"Madeline, what? I'm so sorry that I was an ass to you? That I didn't stick around and see you though your ordeal? That I…"

She sucked in a breath and then bit down hard on her lip to stop herself from talking. "Matt, why did you call?"

"I wanted to see how you were." His voice shook. Her enjoyment of the sound made her feel small.

"I'm fine. I've done four months of chemo. I've lost twenty pounds. I lost all my hair. For four months, I didn't have any breasts, but now I have a nice new set. They're incomplete, but look nice under my shirt. And I have a scar on my stomach where they took the grafting. Other than that, they got all the cancer during surgery. I'm feeling better. My eyebrows have grown in fully, and my hair is coming along nicely."

There was almost a bubble of excitement when she rambled it all off to him. She'd been through a lot in five months. The rest of her life should be a piece of cake.

"And you, Matt? How are you and your new wife?"

"We're fine," he said, and again his voice shook with nerves. Madeline couldn't help but feel a little pleased that he was uncomfortable, just as she'd been when he told her he'd moved on. "The baby was born last week. A little boy."

At the mention of his son, guilt hit Madeline for being so nasty, and she sat back in her chair and let her shoulders fall. "Congratulations."

"Thank you."

"I'll bet he's handsome."

"Oh, yeah. Of course. Eight and a half pounds. He'll be a linebacker," he said on a nervous laugh. "Anyway, I just wanted to see that you were doing well and wish you the best on your continued good health."

"Thank you. Good luck with your son." She paused and then added, "And your new wife."

Her hands shook as she hung up the phone. Rattling off all of her successes over the past few months should have made her happy. Instead she felt empty. Each of the two men she'd vowed to love till death do them part had vowed the same in return and now had moved on. How could she not take that personally?

CHAPTER 37

*A*rmed with her passport and her printed airline tickets, because she never trusted e-tickets, Madeline loaded up her luggage and the kids and headed toward their father's house.

Eduardo sat in the passenger seat, his arms tightly crossed over his chest. "I don't see why you don't just go next weekend when Dad and Kathy are home. It's silly that he wants you there and you won't come," Eduardo continued his assault on her as she drove. This would be the fourth time they'd argued about her timing, but she wasn't cracking. "You've been at every family event together for the past five years. I don't see why his wedding would be any different."

"It just is."

"Well, it's silly."

"When you're my age and your ex-wife gets married, we'll have this talk." Her words were getting sharper, and she knew he'd noticed. However, it didn't stop him.

"You're friends, Mom. Above all else you've always been friends."

"And after this weekend we will still be friends." She tried to smile, but it actually hurt.

He was silent until she pulled into the driveway.

They all piled out of the car and grabbed their suitcases. Christian kissed his mother on the cheek. "Have fun."

"I will, baby. Thank you. Be good for Auntie Arianna."

"We will," he said, smiling.

"I know you will. Keep her in line, will ya?"

"That's more like it." He shook his head and walked toward the house.

Clara wrapped her arms around her mother, and Madeline held her tight.

"I'm going to miss you, Mommy."

"I know. I'll be home in a week. And I'll have a tan and I'll feel so much better, baby."

Clara looked up at her. The apples of her cheeks were pink, and her eyes were soft. "Will you send us a postcard?"

"You bet I will. I'll bring you home something very special. I promise."

Clara nodded and hugged her mother one more time before running up the back stairs and into the house.

Madeline turned around and saw Eduardo lingering at the trunk, slowing pulling his backpack out. He slammed down the door and stood there.

She let out a breath and walked to him. "I'm sorry this is upsetting you. I need to do this."

"I just think it's dumb."

"Ed." She laid her hand on his shoulder. "I can't watch him marry someone else."

"Why? You did it."

"You're right. I did." Embarrassment and anger stirred inside of her. She'd done just that, she'd moved on right away, and it had never felt right. There was only one thing she could say to her son. She had to come clean on why she wouldn't be there. "Ed, you have to understand. I can't even tell you anymore why your father and I got divorced. I don't remember. It just happened.

Everything just got so hard, and we didn't handle it too well. Matt and I grew closer, and when he asked me to marry him, I said yes. I never loved him like I loved your father."

"Well, the two of you should have worked harder."

"Be that as it may, we didn't."

"He was miserable while you were married to Matt."

"I know. I've been told." Guilt stirred in with the embarrassment and anger, and nausea was washing over her.

"Well, you should at least support him."

"I do support him." She knew she had been the one to push him right into Kathy's waiting and wanting arms. Had she not opened her big mouth, perhaps he wouldn't be getting married tomorrow. There was nothing she could do about it now.

She lifted her hand to Eduardo's cheek. He was old enough to understand. "Ed, I love him. I want him happy. Kathy makes him happy."

"Mom..."

"No, don't say anything else. I can't watch the man I love marry someone else." She shook her head, trying to ward off the tears that stung her eyes. "I need you to support me on this. I need you to understand."

She knew he wouldn't accept it, but he wouldn't say anything to Carlos and Kathy either.

He gave her a quick hug. "Have fun." He turned from her and headed into the house.

She'd hoped to make a clean exit without having to see anyone, but when she looked back at the door that Eduardo had just walked through, Kathy stood there smiling.

"I'm sorry you won't be staying for the wedding."

Madeline tried to keep her shoulders down and look less tense than she felt. "Timing was just right for the trip. My boss gave me some extra vacation. I certainly think I deserve it."

"Oh, yes, you do," Kathy said, walking down the back steps toward her.

Suddenly the ring she was wearing around her neck felt heavy. She hoped it was tucked under the edge of her shirt. Damn, she'd meant to take it off.

Madeline cleared her throat. "Everything is set? Last-minute jitters?"

"Like crazy," Kathy admitted and let out a quick breath and put her hand on her chest. "I don't think I've ever been so nervous in all of my life."

"You'll be fine." Madeline's legs were becoming weak beneath her and she clenched her hands at her side to keep Kathy from seeing them shake. "You're getting a wonderful husband."

"Thank you. That means the world coming from you." Kathy turned and looked toward the house. "Why don't you come in."

"Oh, no. That's not necessary. I have to get to the airport," she said, but Carlos walked down the back steps toward them.

"Did she have any luck convincing you to stay for the wedding?" he asked Madeline, lacing his arm around Kathy's waist.

"No." As painful as it was to watch him put his arm around Kathy, she was sure her heart would actually burst if she stayed for the wedding. "I leave in four hours. Sun, sand, and water await me."

Kathy's sister opened the back door. "Kathy, you have a phone call," she shouted from the back door, waving a cell phone in her hand.

"Have a great time," Kathy said, smiling, then she ran up the steps toward the house and disappeared inside.

"Well. I'd better be going." She turned back toward the car and lifted the handle.

Carlos touched her arm. "Please reconsider."

She could feel the tears stinging her eyes. She wouldn't shed them. She'd promised herself she wouldn't.

"I have to go."

"I want you here." His voice was quiet. "You're very important to me."

"Carlos, I was important to you." She watched him wince and she hated that he was hurt by her refusal to attend his wedding, but she couldn't help it. This wasn't the place for her. "I will always be part of your life because I am the mother of your children. But I can't watch you get married."

Carlos closed his eyes and let out a breath. He took a step closer to her, still holding her arm, and opened his eyes. His dark eyes peered into hers, and in them she saw panic, just as she'd seen when she told him she was pregnant the first time. Once she'd have kissed it away, but he wasn't hers anymore.

Carlos looked at the door and then back at her. "Am I doing the right thing?"

"Why are you asking me?"

"Because I need to know it's really over between you and me. Marrying someone else makes that very final."

Madeline swallowed hard. "Yes. It's the right thing." She looked at her bag in the seat and thought of the money she'd spent on the airline tickets. She considered what awaited her if she did go, and what was in store if she didn't. "I have to go. Get married to Kathy tomorrow. Be happy, Carlos. Be happy."

She moved in to kiss him on the cheek, but he turned just slightly and their lips met. As her mouth lingered on his, the moment felt longer than it really could have been. Carlos moved away first, and her heart broke in two.

As quickly as she could she opened the door and slid behind the wheel.

"Be careful," he said, shutting the door, creating a barrier between them.

Madeline backed out of the driveway and headed toward the airport, never looking back. Tears steamed from her eyes and her sobs shook her whole body. She'd given him away, again. This time it was forever.

CHAPTER 38

*A*lone, Kathy sat staring at herself in that dammed mirror in Regan's spare bedroom on her wedding day.

The house was already too full of people, and her dress, so lovely and elegant, constricted her. The rental company had arrived at nine and set up the chairs for the ceremony and the tent and tables for the reception. The caterers arrived at ten, and the florist was finishing the arrangements on the altar and on the tables.

Heidi, Kathy's hair stylist, had driven out for the wedding. She had just finished Kathy's niece's hair and left the room to fix herself up for the wedding.

KATHY'S HAIR WAS PERFECT, HER VEIL WAS THE ONE SHE'D ALWAYS wanted, and the dress... oh the dress. She sighed. She couldn't imagine anything more beautiful. Everything about the day was going to be picture perfect.

The tiny bubble that had started as nerves and stirred into fear began to rise in her chest and settled in her throat as if to strangle her. Everything was perfect, and yet she wasn't happy.

The image of Madeline and Carlos in the driveway the morning earlier had etched its way into her head and had kept her awake all night. She'd watched him kiss his ex-wife. Nothing had ever hurt so badly. It was innocent enough, she tried to convince herself. They'd been married and they remained close friends. She'd had this information going into the relationship, and nothing had changed.

Madeline was a decent person. She'd fought a battle that Kathy hoped she herself never would have to face, and she'd won. A vacation in Mexico was well deserved. And Kathy thought the timing was wonderful.

Oh, she'd have welcomed her at the wedding, and Madeline wouldn't have been obtrusive. She'd have been decent enough to sit in the back, blend with the crowd, and exit almost unseen. Never would she have ruined Carlos' wedding or Kathy's perfect day. Genuinely, she was just that nice.

It should have been a comfort that Madeline had left the country, but it wasn't.

She'd seen Carlos' face when Madeline had driven away.

He was crushed.

He was still in love with his ex-wife.

That strangling fear pushed tears to the surface, and she swallowed them back. He was here, wasn't he? He'd shown up at his sister's house and changed into the tuxedo they had rented. The photographer was with him taking pictures of him and his children, his sisters and brother, and his parents. Regan had given her the update just moments before she'd gone to feed her son, put on her dress, and meet her brother for those very pictures.

Kathy knew she was foolish to be upset. But was it right to be dressed in the dress she'd picked or to actually walk down the aisle? Would he love her like he'd loved Madeline? Was she fooling herself into thinking that her stress was about the wedding?

A tap at the door kept her from processing the question.

Regan opened the door, and she and Arianna walked in dressed in their royal-blue dresses. Regan held a flute of champagne, and Arianna one in each hand.

"We thought you could use this." Arianna handed Kathy a glass.

"Thank you."

"To the future Mrs. Keller." She lifted her glass, and her sister did the same.

Kathy stared blankly at them both and then raised her glass, clinking it against theirs. In a mere hour she would be Mrs. Carlos Keller.

She sipped the champagne, but it was bitter on her tongue and burned her stomach as it landed there like a weight.

MADELINE STOOD BEFORE THE MIRROR IN HER HOTEL ROOM. THE bathing suit Arianna had lent her fit perfectly, and she couldn't take her eyes off her chest. The swells of her breasts were beautiful, and she wanted to weep. She'd been afraid to believe she'd see them again.

Her hair was growing back in, but it stood straight up, only about an inch tall. The wigs she'd brought would be a must. Then again, maybe she'd opt for a colorful scarf under a large-brimmed hat.

A giddy bubble erupted in her stomach. She was about to walk out of her hotel room and sun herself on the warm beach. She'd never done that. The worries and cares that she'd carried on her shoulders for the past year already began to drip away.

Madeline wrapped her head in a bright orange scarf and situated the large, floppy hat on her head. Just for fun, she added a dangling pair of earrings and picked up her oversized sunglasses. She was a sight, she thought. And if she just picked up that book on the bed, her towel, and ordered herself a big, fruity cocktail, perhaps she'd forget that at that very moment, the man she loved was marrying someone else.

CARLOS PACED THE FLOOR IN ZACH'S OFFICE. THE BOW TIE AROUND his neck was choking him.

Zach crossed the room, stopping in front of the liquor cabinet in the corner. He took down three glasses and poured each with two fingers of brandy. He handed one to Curtis and another to Carlos. He picked up his own and held it high.

"To you, my brother. May you be forever happy."

"Ditto," Curtis added.

They all drank down the brandy, and Carlos let it sizzle in his throat. He'd seen family members from both sides filter through the house. His sisters and Kathy's sisters had run back and forth in their blue dresses. Her niece was dressed to match the women, and her nephew looked dapper in his mini tuxedo. But his tuxedo was uncomfortable and confining, and the bow tie was strangling him.

He'd been married; that wasn't making him nervous. He loved Kathy, he was quite certain of it. But what had him on edge was the fact that he couldn't make himself care about the wedding, which was only moments away. All he could think about was Madeline and wonder if she'd landed in Mexico and if she was okay.

"Dad." Eduardo's voice snapped his attention from the empty glass of brandy. "They're ready for you."

He looked at his son, so handsome in his tuxedo. It wouldn't be long before he was the one standing among his family and friends marrying a woman he loved. The thought tugged at Carlos' heart.

"Where's your brother?"

"Right here," Christian said, walking up behind Eduardo. "She looks beautiful, Dad."

Carlos smiled. "I'll bet she does."

He looked around the room. He was surrounded by men who meant the world to him. His brother, his brother-in-law, and his sons. He was a wealthy man.

He wrapped an arm around each of his sons' shoulders and headed toward the backyard, where, with one exception, each chair on the beautiful lawn was filled with someone who cared about him. It was time to move on.

KATHY STOOD AT THE DOOR THAT OPENED TO THE GARDEN, WHERE she would walk among loved ones who had come to see her wed Carlos.

She let out a quiet sigh on the arm of her father. As the doors opened, she saw Carlos at the altar waiting for her.

She had to admit she wasn't sure he'd be there. She'd seen the kiss he'd shared with Madeline the day before, but he'd kept his word. He was here, and all hard feelings drained away as she looked at him, so dapper and handsome flanked by his sons in matching tuxedos. Regan and Arianna followed her niece and nephew down the aisle, and her sisters followed them.

"He's a very lucky man." Her father touched her cheek, and a tear welled in her eye.

"Do you think so?"

"I know so."

Kathy took a deep breath and looked at her beloved. The flutter of nerves hit her stomach again as the harpist began to play, and the guests rose from their seats as her father escorted her toward her husband to be.

CHAPTER 39

*M*adeline had indulged in two strawberry and banana concoctions that had her head swimming. She wondered how she was going to make it back to the room, but then again, she didn't care if she ever got back. The sun was warm, the ocean was welcoming, and the lounge was comfortable. Madeline figured she was as happy as she could be.

"Beautiful, isn't it?" A man sat down in the lounge next to her. He sipped on a bottle of beer and lay back.

"Yes, it is."

"First time in Mexico?"

"Yes."

"On vacation with your husband?"

Madeline tucked in her smile and let the liquor in the drinks numb her to the fact that he was hitting on her. She relaxed and enjoyed the moment.

"I'm not married."

"I'm surprised." He turned his head toward her and lifted his sunglasses. "You are one beautiful woman."

"Thank you." She dropped her shoulders and let the smile surface.

Oh, what would the man think if she took off her hat or he knew she didn't even have nipples under her swimsuit?

"I'm Corbin, by the way." He'd sat up and was extending his hand.

"Madeline," she said, reaching her hand—which she found incredibly numb—and gave him a firm shake, hoping to not be mistaken for just another drunk woman on the beach.

"It's nice to meet you."

He settled back in his seat, and Madeline did the same. No more was said between them for a while. She picked up her book, opened it, and found the words jumped around on the page. She gave herself a little chuckle. Who cared that rum swam in her veins? Sun, sand, and the ocean were at her beck and call. She had no children, husband, doctors, or anyone else who cared, at that moment, what the hell she was doing. They were all occupied at a damn wedding.

Her happy mood turned sour, and she suddenly wished for the cool retreat of her air-conditioned room.

Madeline swung her feet to the sand and started to stand, but the beach was unforgiving on her balance, and she wobbled as her feet sank into the uneven sand. Corbin looked up at her and had already reached out a hand to help her.

"Are you feeling okay?"

She let out a breath. "I think I've had too many of those cocktails."

"Mix those fancy drinks with the heat and they'll get your head spinning."

"As a matter of fact they do." She sat back on the lounge.

"Why don't you let me help you inside."

She contemplated for only a moment. "I would really appreciate that."

Corbin stood and offered his hand. Madeline took it, but when she stood, he pulled her right to him. Her hands rested on his bare arms and her face pressed against his chest.

"You don't drink much, do you?" This was one of those moments a mother would warn her daughter about. There she stood in a foreign country, pressed against a strange man, and she was inebriated. What if he tried to take advantage of her, or steal her money?

"No. I haven't drunk in a very long time. In fact..." She hesitated and then figured she had nothing to lose, and if he was trying to hit on her, what she had to say would have him running. "I've spent the better part of this year on chemotherapy medication. So you can imagine those few drinks threw me for a loop."

He nodded as he wrapped an arm around her, and they began their journey back to the hotel. Madeline had been wrong. Chemotherapy hadn't scared him at all.

"Cancer?" he asked as they neared the lobby.

"Yes."

"You deserve to be on a beach with a drink. I lost my sister last year to breast cancer. Undetected for too long, and we lost her within weeks."

Madeline stopped and looked up at him, her eyes still shielded behind dark glasses. "I'm so sorry."

"Thank you." He opened the door to the hotel and held it open for her.

The cool air was like a drug. The moment it hit her, she felt her pulse slow, and the throbbing in her head began to fade. She slid her dark glasses off and let her eyes adjust to the light inside the lobby.

"Thank you for helping me inside."

"It was my pleasure." He bent toward her and kissed her on the cheek. Madeline felt herself swoon. That wasn't good. She didn't need a man thinking she was an easy vacation fling. She pulled away.

Corbin took a step back. "It would also be my pleasure if you would have dinner with me."

She was sure her face registered her shock by the way his lips curled into a handsome smile. He lifted his glasses from his face and rested them atop his head. His eyes were dark, just like his hair. Sadly, the first thing that crossed her mind was how exotic he looked, much like Carlos. She shook the thought from her mind and looked at the handsome stranger who didn't seem to be put off by her admissions of the last year.

Madeline twisted the strap of her bag around her fingers. Why go on vacation if not to step out of the everyday routine you have? She'd spent the last five years thinking of Carlos every day and what a mistake it had been to let him out of her life as her husband. At that very moment he was moving on and becoming someone else's husband. So why did she have to analyze everything? If this man wanted to have dinner, then she should accept. Maybe, just maybe, she could let herself go a little. Wouldn't it be the brash move she needed if she let another man hold her all night?

She sucked in a deep breath of courage. "Corbin, I would be delighted."

"Good. I'll meet you in the lobby tonight at seven?"

"I'll be there."

He kissed her cheek again, and she turned toward the elevator with a smile. Perhaps she could start all over.

CARLOS LOOKED INTO HIS BRIDE'S EYES. SHE'D SHED A FEW TEARS and he'd brushed them away. If it weren't for the enormous smile she had on her lips, he would have been worried, but she was happy. He knew she was happy.

The minister had asked him if he'd take her for his bride and he'd answered, "I do."

He'd posed the same question to Kathy, who let another tear fall but answered, "I do."

"By the powers vested in me by the state of Tennessee, I now pronounce you husband and wife. You may kiss your bride," the minister said.

Carlos touched her cheek, brushing away the very last tear. He lowered his lips to hers and pressed a soft kiss to them. He felt her tremble beneath him as she wrapped her arms around his neck and took the kiss deeper.

"I would like to introduce you to Mr. and Mrs. Keller," the minister added as the guests applauded.

Carlos took her hand and started back down the aisle. He guided her until they were clear of everyone and back into the house. Then he guided her into Zach's office and shut the door.

She laughed as he gathered her into an embrace and let all the tension that had built in him slide out into a kiss. It was over. He'd moved on and there was no going back now.

"Hello, Mrs. Keller."

"Oh, Carlos." The tears were back in her eyes.

"Please don't cry."

"Oh, damnit. They're happy. I promise they are happy tears."

"Good." He rested his forehead against hers. "You look beautiful. Just beautiful."

"Thank you. I wanted to take your breath away."

"You did." He gently kissed her again. "You sure did."

"The boys look so handsome and Clara, so grown up."

"I was thinking earlier that it won't be long before they are all up there getting married themselves."

Kathy shook her head. "I guess that's the chain of events, right? Cycle of life?"

"That's how it works." He looked up, and through the French doors he could see the guests walking around, being directed by the caterers and attendants. He and Kathy would receive their guests, have pictures, and then the reception would start. "I guess we should see to our guests."

Kathy nodded nervously. Her eyes darted from Carlos to the

door and back. "If you wouldn't mind, I'd like just a moment alone."

He gave her hand a gentle squeeze. "Of course. Don't be too long."

"I'll be right out." She kissed him and he left the room.

KATHY LET OUT A DEEP BREATH, BUT THE AIR STILL BUZZED WITH tension. They'd gone through with it, and he didn't seem to be troubled. But she was. The whole cycle-of-life topic had stabbed her right in the gut. People were supposed to get married, raise a family, and then that family would grow up and marry. But Carlos had pointed out the obvious very subtly—he'd already done that.

His children would in fact begin to drive, go off to college, and meet someone, fall in love, and get married. It would be within the next ten years, not eighteen or twenty.

She tried to still her shaking hands by clasping them together. It was a damn silly time to be worrying about it. But she couldn't help it. It had shaken her up.

They were married. Why couldn't she find the joy in the moment? She was happy, damnit. She was married to the man she loved. It was enough, and she grew angrier with herself for letting her thoughts wander beyond the cutting of the wedding cake.

"Sweetheart, are you ready?" Carlos opened the door.

"Yes. Thank you." She straightened her tense shoulders and willed her unsettled stomach to be calm as she walked to him. As he stepped back to let her through the door, she stopped and looked at him. "I love you. You need to know I love you."

Carlos cocked his head to the side and slid a look over her. "I love you too. Everything's okay?"

"Fine." She balled the fabric of her dress in her fists and forced herself to smile. "Let's go greet our guests."

CHAPTER 40

*A*s the doors to the elevator opened, Madeline saw Corbin standing next to the fountain in the lobby. She wondered if he'd recognize her in her long, flowy dress. Her eyes weren't covered now, and her hair was long and red.

He noticed her and smiled.

"You are stunning."

"Wow. Thank you."

"No, thank you." He offered her arm, and she laced hers through it as they walked to the restaurant.

Madeline had spent the afternoon in her room, wondering if going to dinner with a stranger was the right thing to do. How many times had she seen stories on the news about vacations that ended in robbery or murder? The thought made her twitchy.

"Everything all right?" Corbin turned to her with his bright smile.

All she could do was nod. Stepping out of her comfort level was never something Madeline did well, but after the years she'd spent inside that zone, she thought she'd better learn.

They sat together outside where the terrace overlooked the ocean. The sun dipped down into the water and cast a glow over them. They ate, drank wine, shared conversation, and laughed. The more time she spent with Corbin, the less stressed she felt.

During the evening, Corbin proceeded to move his chair closer to her and now leaned in, touching the softness of the red hair that gave her such personality.

"Why red?"

"My sister-in-law." She sucked back a breath. "My ex-sister-in-law gave it to me to wear. She's an actress in New York and has an entire closet full of these fabulous wigs. She was quite helpful when I needed a pick-me-up." She smiled thinking about it. "My sons like the red one, so I wear it most often."

Corbin sat back in his chair and watched the people as they walked through the restaurant. She wondered what he was thinking. It was obvious to her that he enjoyed people, but why had he picked her out of the crowd? There were hundreds of women on that beach, many with bodies that would fascinate any man.

"So why are you in Mexico," she asked, taking a sip of her wine.

"It clears my mind. Life gets too complicated, don't you think?"

Madeline nodded. Complicated. Yes, that summed up her life lately.

Corbin leaned in toward her. "Have you ever been here?"

"First time."

"I come three times a year. I enjoy the beach, have some nice meals, and relax." He covered her hand with his. "This time I decided I'd find the finest woman on the beach and have a romantic dinner."

Madeline felt her throat tighten. "But you're here with me."

Corbin laughed and sat back in his chair. "And you don't think you're the most attractive?"

"Hardly."

"Not all men seek a woman who looks like she should grace the cover of a magazine. Some of us want that inner beauty and that resonates very loud on the outside as well." He moved his chair around so he sat closer to her. He touched her cheek. "Madeline, you are one very beautiful woman, both inside, and out."

The evening air had grown warmer—or Madeline's blood pressure had taken quite a spike. What did this man want? Was he sincere enough to want only conversation? Or would he expect Madeline in his bed when the evening was over? Was she woman enough to say no? Was she woman enough to say yes?

She took a large drink of her wine.

The waiter took their order.

Madeline mulled over the thought of sleeping with a stranger. Talk about stepping out of a comfort zone; that would do it.

Corbin smiled at her. "You're wondering what my motive for tonight is."

"Is it that obvious?"

"I'm safe."

Of course he'd say that. That didn't help her decide what to do when she was done with her wine and her tilapia.

Their dinner was served and the conversation stayed light. Corbin was a gentleman, and Madeline found she'd eased into the evening and looked forward to whatever might come next.

"There is a piano bar in the lobby. Why don't we go in there, and maybe he'll play us something slow to dance to."

"I think that sounds wonderful."

Madeline gathered her purse and Corbin escorted her from the restaurant.

Just as they crossed the lobby, her phone buzzed in her purse. She dug for it. Her body shook with nerves. Who would be calling her? Something must have happened. Everyone knew she was on vacation.

When she turned on the screen, she saw the text message Eduardo had sent to her. Tears filled her eyes and her jaw tightened. She slipped the phone back into her purse and looked up at Corbin.

"I think I'd better call it a night. Thank you for dinner."

He sighed and dropped his head. "Breakfast tomorrow morning at nine?"

"That would be nice."

"Let me walk you to your room."

She wanted to tell him no. Now wasn't the time to fall apart with a nice man who thought she was beautiful. Why was she mad at Eduardo for sending her a picture of his father and his new bride kissing on their wedding day? She should be happy.

They rode the elevator in silence.

Madeline pulled the key card from her purse as the elevator doors opened, and they walked down the hall to her room. Her hands shook, and she dropped the key.

Corbin bent over and picked it up. "Let me."

He slid the card into the lock and opened the door.

Madeline sucked in a breath and willed the tears away. "Thank you for dinner."

"I had a wonderful evening." He touched her cheek. "I look forward to seeing you in the morning."

With that, Madeline rose on her toes and pressed her lips to his. He didn't move away; instead he gathered her closer to him.

When they'd pulled away, Madeline closed her eyes tighter and thought of the picture her son had sent her. "Corbin, would you like to come in for a drink?"

CHAPTER 41

*C*arlos had fallen into bed exhausted, and as he pried his eye open, he realized he had fallen asleep. He'd probably only dozed off.

He had danced with every woman at the wedding and with Kathy in between each of the other dances. He'd had plenty of champagne and little food, so his head had a dull throb working behind his eyes.

He scrubbed his hands over his face and looked down at the band of gold that adorned his finger. Married. He'd moved on. A little chuckle escaped him. They'd been so tired, they hadn't even consummated their marriage. Well, that wouldn't do.

He rolled over but found that he was alone in their bed.

Carlos sat up and looked around the room. His tuxedo hung in the doorway, the rental bag behind it. Kathy's wedding dress hung on the back of the bedroom door. Really, he thought, those things should have been tossed to the floor in a mad rage. How pathetic was he?

He climbed from the bed and made his way to the bathroom. The small clock on the counter said it was almost eleven in the morning. He shook his head. Perhaps he'd had more champagne than he thought he had.

Carlos brushed his teeth, found a pair of sweatpants and a T-shirt, and pulled them on. He couldn't be sure there weren't people lingering in his kitchen.

As he walked down the hallway toward the kitchen, he noticed suitcases lined up against the wall. A smile formed on his lips. A week in Hawaii. That would be a well-deserved vacation.

Kathy was in the kitchen moving about. He stopped and watched her for a moment. There was an urgency to her. She scrubbed the counters and tucked items into drawers. But that wasn't all he noticed. She was wiping her eyes. She was crying.

He walked to her, rested his hands on her shoulders. She stiffened under his touch. Gently he laid a kiss on her neck. "Good morning, my wife."

She didn't speak. Instead, she brushed away the tears that rolled down her cheeks.

Carlos turned her to him. "Sweetheart, what's wrong?"

"I've made a terrible mistake. I'm so sorry for it too."

"What could you have done? Honey, what happened?" He ran his hand over her hair and waited for her to lift her eyes to him.

"Oh, Carlos. What have we done?"

"Why don't we sit down? Let's have some coffee. I could really use come coffee." He ran his fingers through his hair. "Sit down and I'll make some coffee."

He pulled a chair out for her, and she sat as he busied himself with measuring out coffee and pouring water into the maker. He was fully aware she was sitting at the table tearing apart a paper napkin. On his first day as a newlywed, this was not what he'd expected.

Carlos made himself a piece of toast and found the bottle of Tylenol. He popped two in his mouth and cupped his hand under the faucet to fill it with water to wash them down.

Once the coffee had brewed, he poured two cups, sat down with his toast on a napkin, and looked at his wife. He didn't remember much about undressing and climbing into bed, but he'd slept like a baby. One look at Kathy told him she'd been up all night.

Her skin was pale and her eyes darkened by tears and lack of sleep. He thought the morning after your wedding was supposed to be a happy one. How was it he was afraid to open his mouth?

He took her hand and gave it a squeeze. "Are you feeling okay?"

She released the shards of the tortured napkin and looked at him. "No. No, I'm not okay."

"What did I miss?" He tried to gather her hand again, but she pulled away, setting them in her lap. "Kathy, what is it?"

"We got married."

He gave a little chuckle. "Of course we did. We planned it for months."

"No. What I'm trying to say is, we shouldn't have."

Carlos shook his head. "I don't understand. What do you mean we shouldn't have?"

Kathy dropped her shoulders and stood. She paced the floor for a moment and then dropped her hands and looked down at him. "God, this is so hard."

Carlos rose to meet her eye to eye.

She held up a hand to stop him from moving closer to her. "I was being selfish. I should have called the wedding off weeks ago. But I thought it was the right thing to do, to continue."

He shook his head. He had no idea what was going on. He took another step toward her, but she retreated and walked around the table. She placed her hands on the back of the chair.

"I'm packed and leaving for Hawaii."

"Okay. I'll go get packed." He nodded nervously, motioning toward the bedroom. "Is that what's bothering you?"

"No. I'm bothered by the fact that you won't be going to Hawaii with me. I'm bothered that I let this go this far."

"Where am I going? Sweetheart, what the hell is going on?"

"I'm going to Hawaii without you. Carlos, I don't want to be married."

He moved to her, catching her hand before she could jerk it away. "You're nervous. You don't know what you're talking about."

"But I do." She smiled and let out a breath. "It shouldn't be a problem. The papers haven't been filed. We don't have to file the marriage. It'll be as though it never happened. If they don't accept that, we'll have it annulled."

"You don't love me?"

"Oh, I love you. I love you too much to do this to you."

The breath in his lungs escaped him as he focused on her smile. "What have you done?"

"Stolen you away from the woman you love."

It was Carlos that retreated a step this time and sat down in the chair closest to him. Wasn't she the woman he loved? Kathy was obviously having next-morning jitters. "What are you talking about?"

"Listen, since the day I met you, I knew your heart belonged to Madeline."

Carlos' shoulders dropped, and he was sure his chin had hit the floor. "Kathy..."

She shook her head. "For the past year I tried to convinced myself you loved me more than you love her. But I was wrong. So I'm going to Hawaii alone and you're going to Mexico."

He sat before her dumbfounded. The throbbing in his head increased and so did his heart rate. "Why are you telling me this now? What good does it do me now?" The moment the words hit the air, he wished he could retract them, but it was too late. "That's not what I meant."

She smiled and her eyes began to dry. "Oh, Carlos. You're a good man. Too good to have me as your wife." She laid a gentle hand on his arm. "You and I were trying to fill a hole. We each needed something. You needed to take care of someone, and I needed you to be there for me. You were." She moved past him and paced the kitchen. "Madeline needs you too."

"Kathy."

"No." She raised her hand to stop his protest. "First, I want you to know I'm not upset. This all comes from my heart. But when I watched you say good-bye to her the other day… When I watched you kiss her…"

He stood and she backed away. Oh, he hadn't meant to kiss Madeline. He had to tell her that.

"Please, let me finish." She moved again to create space between them. "Carlos, you need to be with her. And I needed a wedding. I got my wedding, and I'm so sorry to say I was disappointed."

His brows drew together and his lips pursed. The woman had lost her mind.

Kathy picked up the towel near the sink and folded it, he knew, to keep her hands occupied.

"I love you. You're such a wonderful man. But I think you belong with your family, and I should take some time to find the right person for me."

He rubbed the ache in his forehead. Perhaps the champagne still pulsed through his veins, because he wasn't feeling very steady. "Are you standing here in our kitchen telling me, your husband, that you don't want to be married to me?"

"Yes."

He threw his hands in the air. "Kathy, it hasn't even been twenty-four hours. What's wrong with you?"

Instead of crying, she began to laugh. "Don't you see? Nothing is wrong. Except that we don't belong together." She dropped her hands to her sides. "Curtis and Simone had more going on last night than we did."

He'd noticed that his little brother had his hands all over the French beauty, and she'd been reciprocating. Carlos pinched the bridge of his nose, hoping to release the pressure in his head. "Let's give this some time. I'm sure it's nerves."

"No. Nerves got me to this point." She neared him and touched his cheek. "Even I can see that you and Madeline should be together. You love her. It's always been her. And she loves you." She stepped back. "It's been less than twenty-four hours. That's a short enough time that we can tear up the marriage license and send back the gifts." She turned to the kitchen table and picked up an envelope. "I leave for Hawaii in four hours. Then I'm headed to California. I'm going to move in with my sister for a bit and let my life take a new course."

Carlos stood silent. He wasn't sure what to say. This was his wife. He should be stopping her from speaking nonsense, but something was holding him back.

Kathy handed him the envelope. "I had Judy work her travel agent magic. She dropped this off earlier."

Carlos took the envelope and opened it. She'd done what she set out to do, he figured. His stomach began to flutter with nerves at the chance everything was going to be okay. "This is a plane ticket to Mexico."

Kathy nodded. "Go get her. Don't let her go again." She stepped to him and kissed his cheek. "Wow, I can breathe again." She held a hand to her chest. "For the past few weeks I've known this was the right thing to do. I should have done it then, but at least it's done now."

"I can't believe you did this."

"Call your kids. Tell them you're going to go get your wife back." She rested her hands on his chest. "I'm okay. I know you'll worry about that for a long time. That's how you are. But really,

I'm going to be fine. I'm actually giddy about starting over in California."

"I wish I had words."

"A thank-you will do."

He swallowed back the excitement he felt and tried to sound sincere when he sighed, "Thank you."

CHAPTER 42

*C*arlos scanned the people in the hotel lobby as the concierge rang Madeline's room.

The concierge pursed his lips and hung up the phone. "I'm sorry, sir. No one answers. However, many of our guests spend their days out by the pool. Perhaps you'll find her there."

He nodded. He knew he might. If there was sun and water, there was probably a seat for Madeline there.

Carlos walked out of the hotel, in the direction the attendant had pointed. There was large circular bar overlooking the pool, with its thatched roof that shaded those who had come in from the sun. He propped his arm on the bar and scanned the many people sitting in lounge chairs by the pool. She wasn't there. But beyond the pool was a walkway toward the beach, where many more rows of people lay hidden beneath brightly colored umbrellas.

A man walked up next to him in swim trunks and dark sunglasses. "Looks like you just flew in and couldn't wait to get to the beach." The man motioned to the bartender. "Two strawberry daiquiris, please." Carlos felt eyes on him and turned. The guy gave him a quick nod. "Looking for someone?"

Carlos' jaw tightened. He didn't have time to chat with some man who was on vacation. He was on a mission. "My ex-wife." The words, after all these years, were still bitter on his tongue.

"Oh, well, the beach is full of those." The man laughed. "I've been out here most the morning. Maybe I can help you." He turned around and scanned over the crowd. "What does she look like?"

Carlos shook his head. He wasn't in the mood for games. "I don't know."

The man turned back to him. "How long has it been since you've seen her?"

"Not that long." Carlos let out a grunt of a laugh as the bartender placed the man's drinks on the bar.

Carlos twisted Madeline's wedding ring on his pinkie. He'd dug it out of a box he'd kept buried in his closet. He pursed his lips. It never should have been in the box. It never should have left her finger.

Carlos looked out over the sunbathers again.

The man reached for his drinks. "Let's start with the basics. Is she here with girlfriends?"

"No."

"Tall and leggy? Short and curvy?"

Carlos finally smiled. "Short and curvy. Italian with beautiful eyes."

The man nodded. "What color hair?"

"Brown." He shook his head. "Well, wait." He laughed again, this time with ease. "It was brown until we shaved it off."

The man's expression was priceless, but the memory of the day he, Maddie, and Ed shaved their heads made Carlos smile until his cheeks hurt.

"I didn't think this would be so hard." Carlos turned to the bartender. "Two glasses of champagne, please." He turned back around. "Okay. She either has a scarf on her head or is wearing a stunning head of red hair."

The man turned back around, set down his drinks, and held a hand up to the bartender, stopping him from pouring the glasses of champagne.

Carlos turned to the bartender and then back to the man. "Is there a problem?"

The man shook his head and took off his sunglasses. "Not for you."

Carlos ran his hand over the back of his neck. "I beg your pardon."

The man held out his hand to Carlos. "Corbin. Corbin Mason."

"Carlos."

"Yeah. I figured." Corbin put his sunglasses back on. "Madeline?"

Carlos felt the blood drain from his head. Oh, God, he'd never considered that she'd made plans to travel to Mexico with another man. Suddenly the heat and the sun were getting to him. He leaned his back up against the padded edge of the bar to steady himself. The wedding cake from his wedding was the last thing he even remembered eating, and now it was a solid mass in the pit of his stomach.

Corbin looked out over the beach. "She opted for the orange scarf today but left the floppy hat in the room. She's just a little pink from all the sun she got yesterday, but she has a healthy glow." He nodded toward the ring on Carlos' finger. "Planning on dropping that ring into her champagne?"

"Thought had crossed my mind." He turned to Corbin. "Are you here with her?"

Corbin smiled. "We met on the beach and have enjoyed each other's company."

Suddenly the strength of the bar wasn't enough to keep Carlos upright. He sat on the empty stool beside him.

He wiped the sweat from his brow and thought about what

Madeline and this man had been doing together. It wasn't like her, and he assumed that was the point.

Carlos tried to swallow down the bitter taste of regret but found his mouth had gone dry. Add that to the heart ache that squeezed his chest, he thought he might just die on that barstool.

Corbin looked back out over the beach. "In those past few days I've learned a lot about our Madeline."

Our Madeline. The words struck another blow. This man was trying to kill him.

Corbin gave a glance of consideration to Carlos and then looked around behind him. "Where's your wife?"

Oh, the man did know a lot. They'd obviously spent a long time together, probably wrapped up in each other's arms—and sheets. Carlos tried to expel the breath he was holding. "She dumped me yesterday morning."

"She knew you were still in love with Maddie?"

Maddie? He'd already begun with the pet names. But Carlos only nodded.

"Well, then." He handed Carlos one of the daiquiris. "She's grown fond of these. I wouldn't recommend putting the ring in it, though. Perhaps teeter it on the umbrella."

"I don't understand." This man, who had spent time with their Maddie, was giving him advice? Carlos didn't know if he should punch him or thank him. Punching him seemed more logical. Had this guy touched her? The thought made him tense.

"She'll be very glad to see you."

After having met Corbin, Carlos wasn't so sure she would.

"These are on me." He picked up the other drink and handed it to him too. "Give her my best. And good luck to you. She loves you very much, and she didn't have to tell me specifically for me to know."

Corbin gave him a firm pat on the back. "She's under umbrella thirty-three just over there." He pointed in the distance.

"That's it? You can walk away from her like that?"

Corbin put his sunglasses back on his face. "She was never mine. Only for a moment, but never forever."

CHAPTER 43

The sun was hot, and Madeline was glad Corbin had talked her into the umbrella. With its shade, she figured she could spend all day on the beach.

She closed her eyes and let the warmth wash over her. Certainly, the next vacation she took she was going to take with Regan and Arianna. No matter what, they were still her friends, and damnit, she wasn't going to lose that.

With her eyes still closed, she felt the presence of someone standing over her and she smiled.

"I wondered how long it was going to take you," she said, letting out an airy laugh.

He didn't say anything. She heard him set the glass on the table beside her and relax in the lounge.

Madeline sat up and lifted her sunglasses.

The shock of finding Carlos lounged next to her in a white linen shirt and khaki pants gave her heart an unnatural rhythm.

"What are you doing here?" Her skin stuck to the lounge or she would have shot up.

"Soaking in the sun with your new favorite drink." He sipped from his and gave her a sideways glance. "This isn't bad. Corbin said you liked these."

She felt the blood drain from her face as she sat up fully. "Corbin? You met Corbin?"

He sipped from the glass again. "Nice enough guy. I'm not sure I like the thought that he slept with my wife."

"He what?" Confusion would be an understatement for what Madeline was feeling now. "Carlos, what are you doing here and where is Corbin?"

The thin line of a smile on his lips let her know he had something brewing in his head, but then his lips turned downward and he sat up on the lounge.

"Maddie, tell me you don't love the man. Tell me that Corbin was a fling and that you didn't run off to Mexico to be with him."

"Carlos, have you lost your mind?"

"Yes." He let out a breath. "I can't stand the thought of another man touching you."

The man she really loved was sitting across from her accusing her of having some lustful affair. He had indeed lost his mind. What did he think of her? She let her shoulders drop. Why would it matter? She'd contemplated sleeping with Corbin, hadn't she?

"Is that why you're here? You think I'd belittle myself to sleeping around with men I don't know? You think that's what this was all about?"

Carlos shrugged.

"You don't know me as well as you think you do, Carlos Keller."

"Oh, I know you pretty well."

He did too, and that was killing her at the moment. "Then tell me. Did I run down here and sleep with the first man I met?"

Carlos lifted his sunglasses to the top of his head. His dark eyes scanned her face and the smile slowly returned to his lips. In that moment she knew he had his answer. He did know her that well. He relaxed back on the lounge and sipped from his drink again.

Madeline felt the urge to shake the man. Was he trying to torture her because she hadn't gone to his wedding? Why was he here? Why was he ruining her vacation? He should be in Hawaii right now, on his honeymoon, not sipping daiquiris next to her in Mexico. And why was he drinking daiquiris next to her? She swept her eyes over the beach. "Where is your wife?"

"Sitting next to me."

"What?" This time she came off the lounge and he stood to meet her.

He raised his hand to her cheek. "You heard me."

She pulled his hand from her face and looked at it. His ring finger was bare. "Where is your ring? Where is your wife? Damnit, why are you here?"

He moved into her and brushed a kiss across her lips. She was paralyzed. Why could she never move away when Carlos kissed her?

When he pulled back, he kept his eyes locked on hers. "I have been dumped by my wife." He reached for her hand. "We both knew, I'm in love with someone else."

Her breath caught in her lungs and the heat around her swirled until she felt dizzy. Without another thought, she sat down on the lounge, and Carlos knelt down before her, his knee in the sand.

"See, for the past five years it seems that I kept thinking about moving on, but really I didn't want to. You moved on, and so I thought I'd better just do it."

"Carlos, I never moved on." Though she'd sure made a mess of things trying.

He nodded and sat back on his lounge, her hand still grasped in his. "I remember these two foolish kids who got married and had a family. They should have talked more. Instead, they said mean things and lived in separate houses. When really they should have been sharing the same one."

Madeline covered her mouth with her free hand.

Carlos took that hand in his and pressed a kiss to her palm. "You told me you loved me when they wheeled you away for surgery."

She swallowed hard. "Oh, I'd hoped you'd forgotten that."

He shook his head. "Burned into my memory." He smiled. "It stayed there because, honey, I've never stopped loving you. In my heart, you are my wife and always will be. So I don't see any reason we shouldn't be married and pull our family back together."

The picture that Ed had sent her of them kissing had flashed in her mind. "You didn't marry Kathy?"

"Oh, I married her." He rubbed his free hand over the back of his neck and bit down on his lip. "It was a nice wedding."

"Oh." She sighed and tried to sit back, but Carlos didn't release his grip.

"Somewhere between eating wedding cake and waking up the next morning, she decided I wasn't the right man for her. She says we should tear up the marriage license and move on. She's leaving for Hawaii and then moving to California. She had my reservations changed to Mexico so I could come down here and get my wife."

The first tears dropped from Madeline's eyes.

Carlos picked up the other drink he'd set on the table. "I was going to drop this into a glass of champagne."

He held out the glass to her. A narrow band of gold adorned the paper umbrella.

"This is my wedding ring."

He nodded. "Yes. Corbin thought teetering it on the umbrella would be more suited for the drink."

"Corbin?"

He gave her hand a squeeze and locked his eyes with hers. "Tell me you don't love him, Maddie. Right now it would kill me if you told me you did."

She shook her head. "I don't love him. I've never loved anyone but you."

Carlos' shoulders dropped, and the sexy smile that won her over every time surfaced on his lips.

"Madeline, I love you." He took the ring off the top of the umbrella and set the drink back on the table. He took her hand and slipped the ring onto her finger. "Will you marry me again?"

She couldn't answer. She couldn't find the breath to speak. Instead, she pulled her hand back, which was now adorned with the only piece of jewelry she'd ever missed wearing. She turned and reached into her beach bag.

She pulled a chain from the bag and offered it to him, his wedding ring hanging from it.

"I found this the other day."

Carlos fingered the band of gold that dangled from the chain. "You have this with you?"

"I was wearing it around my neck when you kissed me good-bye."

"You kissed me."

"Hm," she laughed. She opened the clasp on the chain and let the ring fall into her palm. "It didn't belong on my neck."

Madeline reached for his hand and slid the ring onto his finger. "It never, ever should have left your finger."

Carlos fisted his hand as if to hold onto the ring. "I love you."

Tears rolled down her cheeks, but she was smiling. "And I love you."

Carlos lifted his hand to her face and brushed away the tears with his thumb. "So, Madeline, will you give me a second chance and marry me?"

"I've never wanted to do something again so much in my life."

He ran his fingers down her neck and over her shoulder, sending a surge of passion and promise through her body. "I'll make you happy."

Madeline lifted her eyes to meet his, and in them she saw his devotion to her. "You always have."

EPILOGUE

$\mathcal{M}$exico would forever hold a special place in Madeline's heart, she thought as she felt Carlos' arm pull her in closer as she woke up the next morning.

Years of misunderstanding and heartbreak had been forgotten as they made love, ordered room service, and made love again.

Madeline looked at the wedding ring on her finger and the matching band on Carlos'. He loved her. She closed her eyes and let the feeling of him wrapped around her sink in.

"I want to say that I never dreamt I'd be in bed with you again, but that would be a lie," Carlos whispered in her ear. "I dreamt about it all the time."

Madeline turned to face him. His face was shadowed with a dark beard, and his eyes remained closed, heavy from sleep. But when they were open, he'd gazed into her eyes lovingly, just as he had since they were young.

Her hair was only a few inches long, her breasts had no nipples, and there was a scar on her stomach, and yet, he'd made her feel beautiful.

"I love you, Carlos," she said and his eyes fluttered open.

"I love you, too." He pressed a kiss to her lips. "Christian is going to cry. Ed will hold in his excitement, but I'll get a high-five later. Clara," he stopped in consideration.

"She'll act like nothing happened at all, and everything is normal."

"I asked Arianna not to say anything to them."

Madeline drew in a deep breath and let it out on a smile. "Mexico is over rated. I think I want to go home."

COFFEE BREWED, PANCAKES WERE MADE, AND BACON WAS COOKED. The aroma filled the house, and was sure to stir sleeping children.

Madeline had wrapped a colorful scarf on her head and adjusted the tie on her robe as she sat at the table sipping a cup of coffee.

Christian was the first to stumble into the kitchen. He rubbed his eyes and sat down at the table before he even looked up. But when he did, his eyes went wide. "Mom! Why are you here?"

Two more wide eyed children turned the corner into the kitchen when they heard Christian's remark.

Clara ran straight to her mother and wrapped her arms around her neck. "You're home."

"I am. I missed you all."

Ed walked around the table and wrapped his arm around her shoulders. "You should have stayed in Mexico."

"I'd had enough sun. Now you all sit down and eat. Then I'll give you what I brought you."

Christian's expression perked up. "You brought us something?"

"I did. Now eat."

Clara and Ed sat down at the table and filled their plates.

When they were occupied, Madeline stood from the table, pulled down another coffee mug, and filled it with coffee.

Ed lifted his eyes, watching her. "You have coffee, mom."

"I know."

"Then what are you doing?"

She only smiled as Carlos walked into the kitchen wearing only a pair of pajama pants. He kissed each of their children on the top of the head, walked around the table, and pulled Madeline to him.

Sliding his arms around her waist, he pulled her close, planting a warm kiss to her lips.

Madeline smiled beneath his lips as she heard the mutual gasps from the table.

Carlos eased back, and she handed him the mug she held in her hand.

"Dad, what are you doing here?" Eduardo asked. "Why are you in your pajamas?"

"You kissed mommy," Clara said with rattle of panic, but then a giggle bubbled from her.

Carlos took Madeline's hand and walked her to the table, where he set down his coffee, sat down in one of the empty chairs, and pulled her down to his lap.

Christian, pushed his plate to the center of the table. "Where is Kathy?" he asked, and it didn't surprise Madeline at all. He would be the first to call out the obvious.

Carlos kissed Madeline again and then turned his attention back to the kids who had stopped chewing mid bite.

"We all make mistakes, guys. Mine was letting this one slip from my fingers."

"Mom?" Eduardo clarified.

"Kathy knew I loved your mom, and she left me."

Eyes shifted to Madeline and her heart swelled in her chest. "We're going to get married again," she said. "Would you be okay with that?"

There was silence for a moment and Christian nodded. "We'd be together again?"

Carlos reached for his hand and gave it a squeeze. "We'd be together again."

"We'd live together?" Clara asked.

Madeline nodded. "Together."

Eduardo crossed his arms in front of him. "You've loved each other the entire time, haven't you? I mean dad couldn't stay away when you were sick."

Madeline pressed her forehead to Carlos'. "Without him, and all of you," she said shifting her glance to her children, "I wouldn't have been as successful in my recovery. But I had everyone who loved me around me."

Eduardo stood and walked to them. Madeline stood and Carlos followed. "You're getting married?"

They exchanged a loving glance.

Madeline smiled. "We're getting married."

Eduardo pulled them both in and Clara and Christian stood and joined them.

"This is the best souvenir you could have ever brought us, Mom," Christian said a he wrapped his arms around her and his father.

Madeline closed her eyes and absorbed the love that wrapped around her. She'd been given a second chance at life and love. Never would she let that slip from her grasp again.

OPPOSITE ATTRACTION

We hope you enjoyed Bernadette Marie's *A Second Chance*.
Continue the family saga with an excerpt from book three,
Opposite Attraction.

OPPOSITE ATTRACTION

*C*hampagne flowed, again.

His brother had married, again.

Curtis Keller knew this marriage would last, this time, but he wondered if he'd ever love again.

He sipped from his glass and watched his brother Carlos dance with the only woman he'd ever truly loved. His Madeline.

Curtis leaned up against the pillar of his sister's porch and watched as couples danced with the bride and groom in the garden. He gave a little chuckle to himself. Carlos and Madeline had been young when they'd first married. No one ever saw it coming, the day Carlos announced that he and Madeline were getting divorced.

She'd gone on and remarried. It had taken Carlos five years to finally remarry, but that had lasted less than a day. Now here they all were celebrating their second marriage, to each other.

Curtis tipped his glass in a toast when Madeline glanced his way. She was a glorious sight and as a doctor, as well as her dear friend, he was happy for her. Only a year earlier she'd been diagnosed with breast cancer. But with a full head of chestnut hair swinging at her shoulders, compliments of his sister

Arianna's extensive wig collection, no one would have ever known that only months earlier Carlos had shaved off all of her natural hair.

His nephews and niece danced among them. His brother-in-law Zach danced with his own mother and Curtis' parents hadn't missed a song all night. In the middle of the dance floor was his older sister Arianna and her date from Carlos' last wedding, and Zach's right hand man in his construction company, John Forrester. They seemed comfortable, as comfortable as you could be with a set-up-date.

As for him, he was happy to watch. The memory of his date at Carlos' last wedding still burned in his gut. Tonight he didn't have an escort, and that was just how he wanted it.

His sister Regan slid up next to him, a glass of champagne in her hand. "You look lost in thought."

He scanned a look over her. "Are you supposed to be drinking that?"

"I won't tell if you don't."

He shook his head. "Expectant mothers aren't supposed to drink."

She nudged him. "Well the expectant father said I could have just a little sip, and since the expectant brother is sleeping I'm not going to worry about it." She lifted the glass to her lips and drank down the bubbly drink. Curtis grabbed her hand and she laughed. "It's sparkling cider. I made sure we had plenty for the kids." She laughed as Curtis settled back against the pillar.

Regan was a wonder to him. There she stood a happy woman married to the man of her dreams. Their son was almost a year old and she was weeks into her second pregnancy. Only he and her husband Zach knew about the baby. She was waiting until after the wedding to announce that she was expecting. She hadn't wanted to take away from the celebration happening around them.

Regan shifted her glance from the dance floor back to him. "You don't seem to be having as much fun at this wedding."

"You didn't arrange a date for me this time either."

With a slow nod, Regan sipped from the drink then handed him her glass. "I'm going to go steal my husband away from his mother."

Curtis watched her do just that and he retreated to the kitchen before Zach's mother Audrey caught him and begged him to dance.

Caterers moved about the house and Curtis fixed himself a plate of fruit. He'd be happier in the kitchen he decided. The reception was depressing him.

When he lifted his head from the platters of food, he saw the reason it depressed him standing right in front of him.

"Hello, Curtis." Simone Pierpont's French accent stabbed right into his heart before he choked on the grape he'd just swallowed whole.

He coughed until he could breathe. Her eyes never wavered from him and he was sure they had bore a hole right through him.

"Simone. I didn't expect you here."

She twisted her fingers together and smiled nervously. "I've been out of town."

Didn't he know that? He'd tried for the past month to find her. Even his brother-in-law Zach, who she claimed was her very dearest friend, hadn't known where to find her.

"You're looking well." He wasn't sure what else to say. He'd been dumped by women before, but it had never hurt like this one did. Oh, she'd had him fooled. Yes, he thought there'd been a chance for something real. He'd thought it was love.

But he had to acknowledge that there were women in the world who appreciated the art of seduction and fast steamy love affairs without stings just as men did. He just never thought he'd be the man who was used and disposed of.

Damn her anyway, he thought.

She took a step toward him and then stopped just short of reaching him. Her knuckles were white now and her nervousness wasn't helping him keep calm.

Simone bit down on her lip then shifted her blue eyes to his. "I would have called..."

"Listen," he set down his plate. "You don't owe me any explanations. Zach and Regan set us up to share the evening together so we wouldn't be alone. They didn't tell us to," he lowered his voice, "screw like rabbits and run off to your yacht in the French Riviera. So we had a good time. Really, who thought much of it?" He had and he fought his eyes to make sure she didn't know how much he'd thought of it.

"Right. It was just sex. I was hoping you would understand that."

"Got it." He picked up his plate. "Well I think I'll go see how the party is going. See ya 'round."

THAT WASN'T EXACTLY HOW SIMONE HAD HOPED THAT WOULD GO. She untangled her fingers realizing they were almost numb now.

She deserved him to treat her like that. She'd been very forthcoming with him, over too much champagne on her yacht, that she'd bedded many men. Why she felt he needed to know that she wasn't sure. She'd left out the hefty part of the tale though. Most of those men had been in her bed while she tried to wrap her head around the fact that Zachary Benson had never seen her as more than a sister or dear friend.

Lucky for her she loved him the same. She was glad he and Regan had found each other and now had a family. But that hadn't changed her view on herself. Simone Pierpont longed for what Zach now had. Love, marriage, and a family. One piece didn't really fit without the other.

She sucked in a breath. Had she not made such an ass out of

herself in front of Curtis and then ran off without a word, stranding him on the Rivera to find his own way home, perhaps she'd have just that.

Simone ran her hands over the slim satin line of her dress, lingering only a moment on her jittery stomach.

Well, she thought, at least she'd have some of what Zach had.

CURTIS LIFTED A GLASS OF CHAMPAGNE FROM THE TRAY AS HE walked out into the garden. He drank it down fast, the bubbles shot straight into his head. As another waiter passed, he set it down and lifted another. He wasn't on call at the hospital for another two days, he'd surly be fine with a few more glasses, especially now that Simone Pierpont had joined the party.

She'd made her way out of the house he noticed. She stood wrapped in his brother-in-law's arms as his own sister looked on lovingly. What an idiot he'd been thinking that it was wise to have whisked her away that night. They'd taken their first tumble right there behind the house.

He drank down that glass of champagne. In all his life that hadn't been his style. What in the hell had he been thinking?

There lay the problem. He hadn't been thinking. Not with his head anyway. He hadn't even realized his brother had been dumped the next morning by his new wife and sent off to find his ex-wife. No he'd fled the country on that damned lovely yacht with a near perfect woman only to come home and find his brother cuddled on his mother's couch with the woman he'd once been married to. Talk about a shock to the system.

He knew there was trouble headed his way when he saw all three of them shift their heads and look at him. Quickly, he finished the glass of champagne and blew out a breath as he tried to focus on Zach walking to him. Things were becoming a bit fuzzy.

"Regan wants me to go in and check on Tyler. Why don't you walk with me."

It wasn't an invitation, Curtis realized, but a request. He followed Zach up the stairs to the small room where his nephew slept. Zach poked his head in and came back with a smile.

"She's a bit paranoid with all these people here, but he's fine."

"Good," Curtis said quickly and turned for his retreat.

"Why don't we go down to the study and have a drink." Zach walked down the stairs and Curtis reluctantly followed. He wasn't sure another drink was a good idea and when Zach shut the door he wasn't sure being in the same room with the man was either.

Zach moved to the liquor cabinet and pulled open the doors. "I got a new bottle of whiskey last week from Ireland. A business associate sent it to me. What do you say?"

Curtis swallowed the words he really was thinking and gave his brother-in-law a nod.

Zach poured them each two fingers full and handed Curtis a sniffer.

"To Carlos and Madeline."

"To them," Curtis said as he threw back his drink and then blew out a fiery breath. Certainly, it was going to take the next two days off work to sober up.

"Good stuff." Zach looked in his glass. "Want another?"

"No." That came out quickly enough he thought. He needed to sit, but Zach was walking around the room as if he needed to talk. Curtis tried to hold on to the ground with his feet firmly planted, but the room was beginning to tilt.

Zach sat on the edge of his desk. "I was surprised to see Simone here tonight, weren't you?"

Curtis shrugged. "Your house. Your friend."

"She sure is. My dearest friend in the world." Zach nodded and then turned his eyes up to him. "She seems a little nervous to be here. She's never been nervous."

He shrugged again, but when his shoulders fell he decided he needed to make it to the couch before the room completely spun on him. "Maybe she's uneasy being her for another of Carlos' weddings." The thought made him laugh. Two weddings in two months was that a record or something?

Zach moved to the seat across from the couch where he'd landed and sat down. "It seems to us she's a little uneasy being around you."

In his current state, Curtis took that as an insult. Fine, if his sister and his brother-in-law thought more of some rich French girl than they did of him. Him, who saved lives every single day. Him, who on occasion, had been known to save his own sister's life, but that wasn't something anyone talked about anymore. Hell, he should be put on a back burner just because of the sexy, leggy, raven haired, blue eyed goddess who seemed to always show up unannounced. He completely understood why *her* uneasiness was a problem.

No, no he didn't.

He tried to focus his eyes. How many glasses of champagne had he had before the whisky? Oh wait, with more thought, he, Carlos, and Zach had already had a few shots before the wedding. No wonder he couldn't focus.

Zach sat back in his seat. "So what went on between the two of you? Simone has never said, and Regan and I have only speculated."

Speculated? Who was Zach kidding? They'd disappeared together for two weeks. Even the hospital was *speculating* if he'd return.

Never in Curtis Keller's entire life had he blown off responsibility as he had with Simone, but damn, it had felt good. It felt good until he woke up on the yacht and she was gone.

The pattern in the carpet was making him dizzy. He looked up and tried desperately to focus on the bow tie of Zach's tuxedo. "I know she's very special to you, but you don't want details."

Zach smiled with a slow nod. "You're right, I don't need details. She is very special and," he looked around the room as if to make sure no one was there. "If you don't mind not telling her I said this, she's a bit of a manizer." That seemed to strike Zach as funny and he laughed. "You know, like a womanizer, only a manizer."

"I got it." But it wasn't funny to him. "What about it?"

"Well we were afraid she dug her claws into you."

That would be an understatement as Curtis remembered it. "Don't worry about me. I'm fine."

"Good. She's going to be staying here for a bit and we don't want it to be awkward for you."

Curtis ran his tongue over his teeth and then did it again. His tongue was numb. "I'll be fine. I'll be working lots of shifts at the hospital so I won't be hanging around here too much." At least not anymore.

"You're okay with her?"

"Sure." Why wouldn't he be? No reason to get worked up just because a woman used you for a quick romp. Really, he was more of a man than that.

"Well I'd better get out to the guests. Feel free to hang here and rest your head."

Curtis acknowledged his generosity with a grunt as he tipped his head back on the couch.

THE HOUSE WAS QUIET WHEN HE FINALLY PRIED OPEN HIS EYES. Someone had laid a throw over him, Regan no doubt. His head was throbbing and his mouth was desert dry.

Curtis swung his feet to the floor and stood slowly. Perhaps the caterers had left something in the refrigerator. He could do with a sandwich on those senseless little rolls they had served.

He stumbled to the kitchen, swung open the refrigerator and

the light illuminated the room. He winced and realized he'd heard a stifled gasp of someone sitting at the table.

Focused on the small figure at the table he shut the door quickly. "Thought I was alone."

"I was hungry." Her face was coming into focus, but the accent alerted him to who the woman in the dark was. She stood and started toward him. "I just came down for a little snack. Can I make you something?"

He'd wanted to laugh as he wondered if she'd ever had to fend for herself in her life. That wasn't fair. Obviously she'd made herself something to eat right there in the kitchen.

"I'm fine. Go finish your snack."

"You're angry with me."

"You think?" He stepped back from her as she approached. That expensive perfume which had tangled with his senses the last time they stood in that kitchen was playing games with his body again.

"Curtis, I'm sorry. I meant you no harm." She moved closer to him in the dark. *"Mon ami?"*

"Friends? Sure." He turned and reached into the cupboard for a glass. At the sink, he filled it with water and felt it land in his stomach. He hadn't slept on that couch long enough to ward of the drunk he'd put on. "Damn," he said under his breath.

"Are you all right?"

"Just hadn't planned on spending the night on my sister's couch. I wanted to get home."

"I'd be happy to give you a ride."

He lifted a brow. "You drove?"

Simone cleared her throat. "You'll be pleased to know I have leased a car. I can drive."

"Hmm, well ain't that something."

He thought he knew her well enough that she'd have had a driver waiting in a car for beck and call.

Even in the dark, he saw her straighten. "You think I'm just some spoiled brat, don't you?"

"Honey, if the high heeled shoe fits..."

Her hand whizzed through the dark and had he been sober he might have had a chance to block it before it hit his cheek. The sting of it raced through his skin and a curse flew from his lips. "Forget the ride. I'd rather walk home."

"Why did I think you had better manners than this? *Ju idiote.*"

She stormed out of the kitchen. If she was going to be around for a while, he'd have a few more chances of pissing her off and that seemed just fine with him. Curtis rubbed at the ache on his cheek.

Well the last thing he needed was for his sister to see him be disrespectful to her houseguest. He'd call a cab. He'd sleep off his drunk and in two days he'd be at the hospital buried in broken bones, cut hands needing stitches, and heart attacks. Suddenly it seemed more appealing than ever.

SIMONE PACED THE FLOOR OF HER BEDROOM. OH, HE'D SET HER OFF and what made her angrier was that she deserved it. Why had she thought things would just fall into place? She had left him stranded on a yacht in the middle of nowhere. She hadn't had the decency to tell him she was leaving or provide for him a way home. Zach had to wire him the money to make it back to Tennessee and she'd heard that he was paying dearly for that at the hospital.

She'd used her wealth to treat him like a prince and then banish him like a pauper. Hadn't he made it clear to her that even though most people thought doctors were self-righteous and rich, he wasn't? Hadn't he told her that he spent more time at the hospital than he did in his little, poorly decorated apartment? Those student loans were plenty and paychecks weren't, he'd said.

But she hadn't expected to fall for him.

Simone looked out over the dark garden from her window and sighed. She'd spent so much of her life trying to be in charge she didn't know what to do when she felt the control slip from her heart. The fact that she'd had many men on that very yacht should have kept things in perspective, but they hadn't. Curtis Keller was the only one who had taken care of her on that yacht and she didn't know how to deal with it.

Sure, many men took care of her. Each of them wanted a piece of what Simone Pierpont could offer them. Curtis Keller asked for nothing.

They'd been thrown together as dates for Carlos' last wedding. They'd met a few times, but once the bubbly started and the music slowed, things changed. She'd changed in his arms that very night and she followed him to that little, rundown apartment he called home, and she'd loved every moment they'd spent there.

Without a bag, she'd worn his shirts around the house. He'd had an extra toothbrush that he'd paid no more than a dollar for that he gave her, and she'd kept. There was no food in the house of the single man and he ordered pizza and over tipped the driver. It was heaven.

Then she convinced him to run away with her for a few weeks. Leave behind the responsibility and the woes of saving lives. Make love to her on the French Riviera under the stars. And so he did.

And that was where she'd left him.

Simone crawled into bed and pulled the sheets up to her chin as if to hide herself in the dark. She'd never been in a situation where she didn't know what to do or have her daddy go fix all her problems. The last time she'd spoken to her father, he'd turned her away. Taken away her trust fund, her villa, everything. To him she was nothing, and he'd made that perfectly clear.

It was hard for her to imagine. Her mother had married,

again, and lived in Spain. And now she couldn't even afford to go to her. Zach had been kind enough to fly her to America and offer her a place to stay. She was sure even Regan didn't know he'd done as much.

He didn't know why she was there, but she'd tell him. And Zachary Benson would never turn her away. That was what friends did for each other.

She'd hoped Curtis wouldn't turn her away either, but it didn't look as though things were going her way.

From the book she bought, she figured she had a good two months before she needed to make her decisions on matters at hand. Zach offered to help her find a job. Why would she need a job, she supposed he wondered. Suddenly an apartment, dark and dank like Curtis', seemed appealing.

It would all be okay.

She was nearing the end of her thirties and she'd never taken care of herself. She could learn.

The first tear rolled down her cheek and she brushed it away.

People did it all the time.

She was good with math. A budget. She could make a budget. Clothing. She and Regan had once been the same size. Perhaps she could talk her into passing down some of the clothes she had yet to work herself into after Tyler's birth. That would do for a little bit.

She blew out a breath and sucked up the tears that continued. She'd learn to take care of another. People did it all the time.

Simone ran her hands over her belly and swallowed hard. Soon Curtis wouldn't turn her away. At least not completely. But she'd have to prove that she could take care of herself before she told him she was carrying his baby.

PLEASE REVIEW

We hope you enjoyed *A Second Chance* by Bernadette Marie. If you did, we would ask that you please rate and review this title. Every review helps our authors.

Rate and Review: A Second Chance

ABOUT THE AUTHOR

Bestselling Author Bernadette Marie is known for building families readers want to be part of. Her series The Keller Family has graced bestseller charts since its release in 2011. Since then she has authored and published over fifty books. The married mother of five sons promises romances with a Happily Ever After always...and says she can write it because she lives it.

Obsessed with the art of writing and the business of publishing, chronic entrepreneur Bernadette Marie established her own publishing house, 5 Prince Publishing, in 2011 to bring her own work to market as well as offer an opportunity for fresh voices in fiction to find a home as well.

When not immersed in the writing/publishing world, Bernadette Marie can be found spending time with her family, traveling (mostly to Disney parks), and running multiple businesses. An avid martial artist, Bernadette Marie is a second degree black belt in Tang Soo Do, and loves Tai Chi. She is a retired hockey mom, a lover of a good stout craft beer, and might have an unhealthy addiction to chocolate.